ORDER OF THE BROKEN BLADE: BOOK 4

CECELIA MECCA

ALTIORA PRESS

THE EARL Copyright © 2020 by Cecelia Mecca

Cover Design by Kim Killion @ The Killion Group, Inc.

Edited by Angela Polidoro

ABOUT THE AUTHOR

Cecelia Mecca is the author of medieval romance, including the Border Series, and sometimes wishes she could be transported back in time to the days of knights and castles. Although the former English teacher's actual home is in Northeast Pennsylvania where she lives with her husband and two children, her online home can be found at CeceliaMecca.com. She would love to hear from you.

ALSO BY CECELIA MECCA

Order of the Broken Blade

The Blacksmith

The Mercenary

The Scot

The Earl

Border Series

The Ward's Bride: Prequel Novella

The Thief's Countess: Book 1

The Lord's Captive: Book 2

The Chief's Maiden: Book 3

The Scot's Secret: Book 4

The Earl's Entanglement: Book 5

The Warrior's Queen: Book 6

The Protector's Promise: Book 7

The Rogue's Redemption: Book 8

The Guardian's Favor: Book 9

The Knight's Reward: Book 10

Border Series Box Set 1 (Books 1-3)

Border Series Book Set 2 (Books 4-6)

Enchanted Falls (Time Travel)

Falling for the Knight

Bloodwite (Contemporary PNR)

The Vampire's Temptation

The Immortal's Salvation

The Hunter's Affection

CHAPTER 1

"The barons and King John could scarcely have imagined when they stood in this meadow 800 years ago today that the words to which they agreed would launch the progression of the rule of law. In this field were born precepts that made possible the United States Constitution, the United Nation's Universal Declaration of Human Rights, and the framework of justice in America, the United Kingdom, and much of the world."

~ *Atty. William C. Hubbard*

LICHEFORD CASTLE, *England, 1215*

"Nude becomes you, Lady Threston."

Conrad, as always, told only the truth. She was quite handsomely formed for a woman of two and thirty or, more accurately, for a woman of any age.

"Jeanette," the blonde widow corrected, not for the first time that evening. Or since they'd met the month before. It peeved her when he used her courtesy title. "Come back." She bent one leg up slowly, giving him a view sure to entice most men.

But not him. Not now.

"I cannot."

Conrad could have told her his steward awaited him. Or that he was so anxious for word from his friends and co-conspirators at Dromsley Castle that he felt the need to keep a near-constant lookout. He'd not heard from any of them in more than a fortnight. But taking her into his confidence in such a way would deepen their relationship, something he had no intention of doing. So instead he said nothing and continued to dress.

"I spoke with your guest, Lady Sabine, today." Jeanette lowered her leg, though she did not attempt to cover herself, another attribute he quite liked. Her lack of modesty became her. "She speaks to me as she would any other widow of my station."

"I'm glad for it." Conrad finished wrapping the laces of his boots and stood.

Unfortunately, he seemed to have missed her point. Jeanette's perfectly arched eyebrows turned downward, but she did not comment.

Conrad relented, if only slightly. "Jeanette?"

He stood by the bed, waiting.

"I am not simply any widow at Licheford."

Ahhh. She wanted him to openly acknowledge her. That was something he could never do, not for her or any woman. He had been clear about his limitations that first night, but Conrad had suspected for some time now that Jeanette wanted more from him. They would obviously need to have a talk. On another day.

"You are a most entertaining bed partner." Conrad leaned down, kissed her, and stood to leave. "But one who must do without her earl for the evening. We will talk more on the morrow."

Surprisingly, she held her tongue, although she was clearly unhappy with his dismissal.

He should not have come to her.

But the waiting . . .

Making his way from Marchette Tower toward the keep, Conrad looked for Wyot. Thankfully, his steward's red hair should be easy to spot, even in the crowd dispersing from the evening meal he had missed.

"I'd not have expected you back so soon."

It was Guy's voice. If anyone was more impatient for news than Conrad, it was Guy. As a mercenary who had also been raised by a mercenary, he was accustomed to moving from place to place. The months he'd stayed at Licheford, waiting for word—from their friends, from the king, from anyone—would likely have driven him mad if not for Sabine. Although his friend had once spurned marriage, he had found the one woman who suited him.

He turned toward his friend, fully expecting a joke about his failure to make an appearance at the meal.

"Oh?" he asked. Then, because he couldn't help himself, he added, "Any word?" He'd asked Guy that very same question just before his short visit to Jeanette.

Guy rolled his eyes. "Aye, in the very few moments you've been gone—a fact that does not recommend your manhood, my friend—we have indeed received word. A missive from Dromsley."

His mocking tone said otherwise, but Conrad decided to play along.

"And what, pray tell, did the missive say?"

The sound of childish laughter drew his gaze to a couple of young children playing with a pup in the corner of the courtyard. Conrad would fight to preserve their innocence, their smiles and laughter. The king's unjust policies and cruel taxes and reprisals, all to fund a war no one wanted, had taken a toll on the country he loved. They had not touched Licheford yet, but if King John went unchecked, they would. He and the other members of the order had set out to stop that. They, along with the twenty or so barons who'd joined their cause, had taken the unprecedented step of presenting the king with a list of demands. He had indicated he would treat with them, but they'd heard nothing else. All winter they'd waited for a response.

It was enough to drive a man mad.

"It was quite surprising, really," Guy continued. "It said your continued vigil for a missive is likely to drive away your friends, your steward, that lusty widow, and all those who come into contact with you."

Conrad crossed his arms. "I do not fare well with all this waiting," he admitted.

"I had not noticed."

"My lord?"

Wyot pulled on his bushy red beard as he approached them, a sure sign he had something important to impart. The steward bowed to them, his back slightly hunched with age, a habit he persisted in despite the fact that Conrad had long ago entreated him to stop.

"A party approaches," Wyot said.

Conrad waited for more information, his heart beating out of his chest, but the steward didn't seem to be inclined to offer it. "Who?" he finally asked, running his hands through his hair.

"We do not know yet."

Conrad had waited all winter, preparing the men. Preparing to defend Licheford against siege or an attack.

Preparing for war.

Perhaps he was foolish, but he would wait no longer.

"I will meet them," he said, striding toward the door that would lead to the first floor and outside the keep. He could feel Guy's presence behind him, but Conrad did not slow his pace.

Finally, the waiting had come to an end.

CHAPTER 2

This was the moment Cait Kennaugh had been thinking about, dreaming of, for so many years.

Though two tall, well-built men approached the gatehouse, first on horseback and then on foot, she knew which one was Conrad before their faces came into view. She would have recognized him anywhere. The young man of ten and nine was now less than one year shy of seeing his thirtieth summer. But his features remained the same.

A slightly squared jaw and thick eyebrows, now furrowed in confusion. Even back then he'd approached her as if the entire tournament were his for the taking. She may have thought him the King of England himself if the king were but twenty years younger. Cait had never actually seen the man, or the Scottish king either, for that matter, but she had always imagined royalty would walk that way.

More than ten years later, his gait was still the same. As if he'd been given a divine right to rule over others.

Aye, she'd know him anywhere. Conrad had

stopped to speak to her brother, but he was looking at her.

"Are you well? The color has gone from your cheeks." Roysa said in an undertone after she greeted Terric and came back to check on her.

Cait could have lied, but there was no use for it. Her friend had only to look at her hands, visibly shaking even though they were gloved and gripping the reins, to know she was anything but well.

"Nay."

"*Oh.*"

Tearing her gaze from him, Cait directed her attention to her sister-in-law instead.

"Of course. I had not considered . . ."

Trailing off, Roysa looked back to the men, who were now greeting each other like brothers. Which they were, of a sort. Friends bonded by an event that had forever changed their lives.

And hers.

Roysa had become the sister Cait had always wanted, having been raised with two brothers. She'd considered telling her friend the truth about why she'd come to England, but something had always stopped her. Even now, faced with his presence, she couldn't find the words.

The hero who had saved her life.

The only man she had ever loved.

"Is that the mercenary with him?" she asked instead.

Roysa stood on her toes. "I cannot see whilst on foot."

Cait had only met Sir Guy once, that same life-changing day, but from the warmth with which her brother greeted Conrad's companion, she suspected he was indeed the fourth member of the Order of the Broken Blade.

"Roysa," Terric called to his wife, motioning for her to join him again. But she stayed where she stood, staring at Cait with concern in her eyes.

"Go. I am fine," she lied.

Roysa blinked.

"Nay, you are not fine. I will be back."

She tried to argue, but Roysa had already walked away. Cait watched mutely as Terric introduced her to Conrad. They spoke for a moment longer and then all turned toward her.

Panic seized her throat and squeezed.

She'd asked, nay begged, to be here. Both of her brothers had wanted to keep her safe from the danger that danced around them, and yet she'd insisted on being here. She'd come to Licheford for one reason, and now that she was here, Cait simply could not do it.

She couldn't speak to him just yet. Even seeing him from this distance . . . she struggled to control her own heartbeat. Struggled to breathe.

I should not have come.

When her brother mounted, preparing to ride through the gatehouse and onto the castle grounds, she assumed Roysa would do the same. Though she'd never been to Licheford Castle, it was obviously larger than most. It would be quite a distance yet to the keep.

"I ride with you," Roysa said, walking toward her with purpose in every step. "A squire will lead my horse."

Cait hardly had the opportunity to move her foot from the stirrup before Roysa used it to hoist herself up, lifting her arm for Cait's assistance, and slid onto the saddle behind her.

As she seemed to do each day, Cait gave silent thanks to the saints for having brought Roysa into

Terric's life. Her brother was extremely lucky to have such a wife, but she considered herself just as lucky. Roysa knew her well enough by now that she did not ask any further questions.

"Is all well?"

The question came from Roysa's sister, Idalia, who'd ridden up alongside them. Idalia was married to Lance, another member of the order. Without them, Roysa and Terric would never have met. Although Cait didn't know her as well as she did Roysa, she was grateful to her for that fact alone.

"Aye," she answered.

"Nay," Roysa answered at the same time.

Idalia looked back and forth between them and said nothing. Although she might press Roysa for details later, she must have seen something in Cait's face that had silenced her. None of them spoke as they rode across the drawbridge, its moat deep beneath them, the clanking of horses' hooves all around.

Grateful for the sisters' companionship, and slightly calmer for it, Cait allowed herself another glance. His back was to them now. Even so, she could not look away from the long, muscular line of it. How many times had she lain awake at night imagining how he had changed? Or how he might react were they ever to meet again?

The timing could not be worse. They were in the midst of a rebellion. One missive away from war with the King of England and his many supporters. Her brothers, this once, had been right. Cait should have stayed at Bradon Moor. Stayed safe in Scotland.

Pleased her mother. Married Colin MacGregor.

She should have done many things, but instead Cait was here, riding toward an uncertain future, painfully aware how little her presence was needed.

I should not have come.

"It must be difficult," Roysa whispered.

She nodded, allowing her to assume that seeing Conrad had brought back memories of that day. Which of course it had. Just not *that* memory.

* * *

Fourteen years earlier

"TERRIC MENTIONED his sister had made the journey."

Conrad bowed even though his station did not require it. There were so many sights and sounds competing for attention, from the clanging of practice swords around them to the flags of every color flapping in the wind atop the tents, that Cait pretended to be unaffected by the Englishman and his pretty manners. But it was just that, a pretense.

At ten and five and a Scottish noble, Cait had met many handsome men, potential suitors, at Bradon Moor, and none had dared to look at her quite so boldly as this Englishman. Maybe because they were too afraid of her father and brothers to approach her with confidence.

Indeed, Terric made his displeasure known immediately.

"He mentioned other things as well"—her brother cleared his throat, not so subtly chastising the earl's son—"about the sister."

Accustomed to her brother's protectiveness, she ignored Terric's clear warning.

"Oddly, he said nothing of you," Cait lied, smiling. Indeed, it had been the opposite. The year before, her brother had returned from his first Tournament of the North full of tales of English knights and bloody melees. And he'd spoken of one young man in particular—an earl's son who had come to his defense against the inevitable slurs his countrymen had made against the young Scot. Never mind that the purpose of the yearly tournament was to bring the two sides together.

She'd heard of Terric's new English friend many times, in fact, and when her father had finally relented, allowing her to attend her first tourney, Conrad Saint-Clair, was one of many sights she'd looked forward to seeing in the south.

And see him she did. It would have been difficult for any girl to miss him. Unlike her brother, who looked very much his age, the earl's son appeared as if he were already a man fully grown. Neither was she the only girl at the tourney to notice him.

"Then I will strive to ensure your memory of me proves stronger than your brother's," Conrad said, his voice thick and deep. The look he gave her then prompted her brother to later proclaim she could not be alone with the Englishman—and it prompted her to seek him out despite Terric's decree.

It was that look that had told her, for the first time, that Conrad liked her.

And Cait very much liked him back.

* * *

OPENING her eyes and cleaning memories of the past as her mount slowed to a stop, Cait forced herself not to recall what had happened next. How the sweetness of those first moments had soured so quickly.

When they reached the stables, Terric stalked toward them, already on foot. So he'd noticed. She'd thought he might. Terric could be strangely perceptive, after all, and he knew both her and Conrad well

11

enough to have sensed the strangeness of the look they'd shared. He offered his hand to her.

"Cait," he said.

"Brother," she replied evenly. "You may wish to assist your wife in dismounting first."

Roysa had already grasped Terric's outstretched hand, but for the first time since they were married, he barely seemed to notice his wife. His glare was fixed on Cait.

"Your turn," he growled.

Reluctantly, she took his hand, his firm grasp yet another indication that he intended to give her a talking-to.

"It seems we have much to discuss," he said for only Cait to hear. Roysa, perhaps sensing the tension between them, had stepped away to speak with her sister.

"Indeed," she agreed, although she had no intention for that conversation to happen just yet.

There was someone else she needed to speak with first. And Cait could wait for it no longer.

CHAPTER 3

She was here.

Cait was here, on his land.

If King John himself had greeted him at the gatehouse, Conrad would have been less surprised. Less unsure. He'd convinced himself Cait was part of his past, that he would likely never see her again, and yet, here she was, being helped down from her mount by the very brother who'd demanded answers from him just moments before.

"Why do you and Cait look at each other so?" Terric had said.

As if he had any answers to give.

Conrad watched, mesmerized, as Cait handed her reins to a stableboy and began walking toward him. In the short time it had taken them to enter the castle walls, darkness had begun to fall, the light of day quickly waning. Attempting to distinguish her features anyway, he didn't move.

"If Conrad will not properly welcome you to Licheford," Guy said alongside him, slapping him on the shoulder jovially, "allow me to do so in his stead."

Reluctantly, he looked away from Cait, toward his other guests. Lance and Idalia and Terric.

"Who would have suspected a mercenary might have better manners than an earl?" Guy quipped. "Come, warm yourselves. We've been waiting patiently for you. All except for our friend here"—he clapped him on the shoulder again. "No one would call him patient."

Conrad forced a laugh, allowing his friends to lure him into the castle, but before he entered the keep, he glanced over his shoulder one last time. He hoped to catch her eye, but she was gone.

At least, he did not see her among the others.

"Conrad?"

It was Guy, no doubt trying to goad him into being a host to his own guests. His friend had a slightly puzzled look.

"For a mercenary, you do quite well," he said, although he could hardly focus on anything but Cait. For weeks, he could think of nothing but receiving word from these very men—their brothers—but now, word from the north was only one of his concerns.

"Come inside," he said, stepping over the threshold. The entranceway opened directly into the great hall, a rarity for a castle of this size, but they'd already climbed a set of stone stairs outside. Conrad had hardly noticed them.

His steward greeted the guests as Sabine rushed forward to embrace Idalia. Everyone began speaking at once, and for a moment Conrad thought he could perhaps slip away and find her, but a hand grabbed his arm.

"Shall we have that talk?" Terric asked, his voice brooking no refusal.

Conrad had hoped to speak to Cait before being cornered by her brother, but there was no help for it. Leaving the group in Wyot's capable hands, he shrugged off his friend's hand and led him down the long corridor to the south solar. Larger than the other solar abovestairs and, unusually, located on the ground floor, it was the chamber in which Conrad spent most of the day.

A smaller version of the great hall, similar in shape and structure, the chamber received some light in the daytime courtesy of small windows, but not nearly as much as the lord's solar. The one Conrad still couldn't bring himself to use.

"Guy and Lance will be along."

Terric glared at him. "Aye, likely they will."

"We've much to discuss."

Terric crossed his arms. "Including the reason my sister risked her life by coming to England now after refusing to do so since . . . then. Since the tourney."

"She gave you no explanation?" Conrad asked.

In answer, Terric merely raised his brow, waiting for him to speak.

"I am as surprised as you to see her," he said honestly, though he stumbled on the word *surprised*. A rarity for him. He spoke three languages, wrote in four, and never had difficulty summoning the right word. His parents had raised him as the sole heir to Licheford, but the best tutors in all of England could not prepare a man for a situation like this one.

"As surprised as the rest of us to find my sister looking at you as if you were a spirit raised from the dead?"

"She came with Rory," he guessed. It was the only explanation for why Terric was here and not at Dromsley, especially given that Cait Kennaugh would have needed someone to escort her across the border. He would not have left his estate with anyone else at such a time.

"Aye," Terric confirmed.

The wooden door scraped open.

"So kind of you to receive guests by absconding away without us," Guy said. Since he knew nothing of Cait, Conrad could not blame him for his confusion. After all, he had been an abysmal host—his mother would be ashamed of him.

Lance followed Guy into the room, not bothering with any preliminaries or pleasantries. "Talk to us."

Conrad had to smile at that. Lance was the most direct of all of them, even more so than Guy.

"Ask him." Conrad nodded to Terric.

"Me?" Terric's eyes narrowed.

If Cait had not said anything about their . . . connection on the way to Licheford, Conrad would not betray her by speaking out of turn. Terric must have realized it, for he frowned, grumbling something none of them could hear clearly, and sat in a high-backed wooden chair.

Lance and Guy said nothing.

"He does not appear to be forthcoming with information." Guy sat on the chair next to Terric. "Though we are glad you are both here, are we not?"

The question was directed at Conrad, who forced himself to nod.

Frustrated and eager and so very tired of waiting, Conrad felt a familiar urge to lash out. Instead, he tended to the fire that was nearly always ablaze in the corner of the room.

The members of the order had never been at odds before. Not even when he'd suggested they form an order to rebel against their corrupt king. The four of them had an unshakable bond, formed at the Tournament of the North these many years past. Together, they'd saved Cait from being raped. Together, they'd killed the king's man.

It was on that day that he and Terric had first met the mercenary and the blacksmith.

Now he felt as if he were on shaky ground with his friends. His brothers. He should have told Terric the truth about Cait sooner. But he'd feared it would change everything between them.

That could not happen. Not now. They needed to pull together, not fall apart.

I have to speak to Cait.

"This is about your sister." Lance sat, leaving Conrad the only man standing. It was a comment, thankfully, and not a question, and neither he nor Terric seemed eager to respond.

Guy filled the awkward silence as Conrad leaned against the stone wall, unable to sit still.

"What happened? Do you have news? We really have been desperate to hear from you."

"Dromsley was attacked." Terric spoke as if such a thing were a regular occurrence. His scowl indicated his mind was still fixed on Cait.

Guy sat up. "Attacked? By whom?" he asked.

"Details, brother," Conrad insisted, the moniker leaving his lips before he remembered Terric was not happy with him at the moment.

"About my wife, or about the battle?" Terric asked, smiling for the first time. "I'll bet neither of you ever thought Lance and I would become brothers in truth."

Brothers in truth. Something about that phrase bit into Conrad, but he shook it off. Although he was happy for his friends, he thought it a rather inopportune time for them to have decided marital life was agreeable.

"I've offered my congratulations," he tried again, "but I'd like to hear more about the attack."

Patience was not Conrad's most endearing trait. In fact, he had very little of it.

"Roysa came to Dromsley just after she was widowed, looking for Idalia. It was through her we learned her brother-in-law, the new lord of Stokesay, conspired to march on Dromsley."

Ulster, a notorious king's man. It did not surprise him. Nor was he surprised to learn there had indeed been an attack. The order had expected that either Dromsley or Licheford would take the brunt of King John's ire. Given that he and Terric were two of the four men who'd started the revolt, and the others were staying with them as guests, they were natural targets. Luckily, both castles were also well fortified.

"Bastards, both." Guy crossed his arms. "We suspected something like this. I'm not surprised to learn John never intended to meet with us. He simply wanted more time to act."

"What happened?" he asked of Terric again.

"'Tis a long story," Lance said, clearly weary. "We prepared for siege but found ourselves in battle instead." The blacksmith smiled. "And we won."

Guy's laugh was what all four of them needed. "That you're sitting here is evidence of it. But more details would be welcome."

"And will be forthcoming," Terric cut in. "Tomorrow. I am hungry. And tired."

"And newly married." Guy winked at his friend. "Lady Roysa is a lovely woman."

All three of them glared at the mercenary. His smile slipped slightly. "Is she not? I meant nothing inappropriate. I'm a happily married man myself."

Aye, she was lovely, but not so lovely as Cait. Conrad wanted to see her. Needed to see her.

"Shall we dine, then?" Conrad asked. "I missed the evening meal myself."

"You should tell them why," Guy prodded. "Or perhaps the lovely Lady Jeanette will be lurking in the hall, looking for you."

Jeanette.

If Conrad had possessed the ability to silently murder a man with his gaze, Guy would be the first one to know about it. In his typical fashion, the marked man grinned back at him as if he were the cleverest person in the chamber.

Indeed, he could be right. But he was a bit of a bastard too.

Conrad avoided looking at Terric, but he could feel his friend's eyes on him.

"We will talk more," Conrad said, pushing away from the wall. "But first, we eat."

CHAPTER 4

"You won't come down?" Roysa asked, dejected.

"Nay, I'm not hungry," Cait said, which was true enough.

"But you've not eaten since this morn." Also true, although her stomach would not hold down any food. She felt quite sure of that.

Cait played with the ties on her kirtle, avoiding the other woman's gaze. Roysa had refused to sit, so the two of them stood in the middle of Cait's chamber, unmoving. What it lacked in light, the small but beautifully decorated room made up for in finery. Everywhere she looked, scarlet and gold dominated. The bed curtains, the tapestries. It was as fine as any lady's chamber, and Cait could not help but wonder who resided here normally.

"Well, if you aren't hungry," her friend said, "will you at least tell me why you were looking at the Earl of Licheford as if he were the first course in a splendidly delicious meal?"

They had been installed in separate chambers, but Cait was just two rooms away from Roysa and Terric, in the same tower. Despite its size, the keep at

Licheford Castle was fairly easy to navigate. A square with four towers, and they were both guests in the one facing west. Unfortunately, it was also the closest to the outer wall, which meant no large windows, but there was plenty of light from the hearth and the candles spread about the room for her to see Roysa's very determined expression.

But Cait was even more so.

Until she spoke to Conrad, she simply did not wish to discuss her feelings for him.

"I thought at first you seemed unsettled just to see him, and his scar . . ." Roysa trailed off. The scar along the right side of his face, from cheek to chin, had been the price he'd paid for saving her. "But I can tell there's more to it. I know you too well to think otherwise, though not as well as I would like." Roysa paused, then added, "You came back to England for him? For Conrad?"

So accustomed to avoiding questions, to changing topics, whenever discussion turned to the tournament, Cait's instinct was to do the same right now. But her sister-in law seemed so eager to help her, to know her better.

She could give her at least this much.

"Aye," she said simply, and instantly regretted it when she saw the pity in Roysa's eyes.

"Do not look at me that way. This has naught to do with the attack."

And yet she felt weak again. Helpless. She'd felt so brave following Rory to Dromsley. For not allowing herself to be sent back home.

But now that she was here . . .

She couldn't go down to the great hall to join the others. Not yet. She wasn't ready.

"Come," Roysa urged, motioning to the door. "It

will be a joyous reunion, all four of the men. You can meet Sabine."

"We met briefly earlier."

"You need to eat."

Roysa's shoulders sagged when Cait shook her head.

"I am not hungry," she insisted again. "Go, tell Terric I will speak to him on the morrow."

Roysa arched her brow. "And the others?"

"Do you mean Conrad?"

Roysa blinked. "Perhaps."

There was no message she could offer to explain her actions. She needed to speak with him, but not tonight. Not in front of the others.

"Nay."

Roysa must have sensed she'd say no more. With one final frown, she turned toward the door. "Shall I have someone sent to assist you?"

Cait glanced down again at the ties on the sides of her kirtle. "Nay," she repeated. But just before her sister-in-law shut the door, she added, "Thank you."

"Good eve," Roysa murmured, closing the door behind her.

Roysa's warm smile reminded Cait of her closest friend back home. She missed Cristane dearly and hoped they would soon be reunited. Cait stared at the closed door for a moment, taking note of the vines that had been etched from the top of the door all around its edges. It took a skilled woodworker to create such a thing. Her chest heaved as Cait imagined those vines coming to life, winding past the door and around the stone walls. Closing in on her.

Pushing the thought from her mind, Cait removed her kirtle and undertunic and washed using the basin of rosewater that had been set out for her. She pulled her hair back, tying it off with a white satin ribbon, and sat in front of the hearth in her robe. It was warm, aye, but still a shiver ran down her back as she thought of him.

Just belowstairs.

It had been foolish of her not to go with Roysa. If her purpose was to avoid Conrad, she could have easily done so by staying in Scotland.

You would be married by now.

Closing her eyes, Cait took a deep breath and then another. She willed herself to stand, to make her way to bed, but decided she would sit for just a moment longer, rest her eyes for a bit.

Cait jumped from her seat, one glance at the fire telling her she'd fallen asleep.

A knock landed on the door, heavy and sure.

CHAPTER 5

Terric would be furious if he found him standing outside Cait's bedchamber. Throughout the evening meal, he'd caught his friend watching him, and even though her name had only been spoken once—when Roysa had conveyed that she would not be joining them—Conrad had no doubt she would be the first topic of the order's conversation in the morning.

And he was still unsure of what to say.

And so, he'd made a hasty, and possibly dangerous decision, and had come to her in the night.

He knocked again, his need to talk to her stronger than his aversion to possibly waking her from sleep. Conrad simply could not wait any longer.

Cait Kennaugh was here, behind this very door.

It opened.

As she came into view, Conrad tried to remember to breathe normally. If he'd thought Cait uncommonly lovely as a young woman, and he had, she was even more so now, though markedly different. Her face was thinner, though still strong. Or was it the look in her deep brown eyes, which rounded at the sight of him?

Her hair, though pulled back, was much shorter as well.

But her set jaw was as strong now as it had been then, and there was no mistaking the determination in the shape of her brows . . . Aye, Cait Kennaugh was every bit the woman he remembered.

"Conrad."

Her voice hadn't changed either. Light and slightly breathy as if every word was pulled from her depths—a land he knew he'd never return from if he dared to visit.

Conrad had known it then, and he knew it now.

"You did not come to the hall."

An inconsequential thing, really, given all of the unsaid things that swam between them. But although Conrad was an earl, trained for years to become one, this woman made him feel like an untrained squire. A boy surprised to find the blood of one of the king's most treasured advisors on the tip of his sword. A boy who cared more for the safety of a young woman he'd just met than for himself, or the fact that he was in very real danger of discovery, and reprisal, for what he had done.

"I . . ."

A sound in the passageway distracted her, but Conrad did not flinch. The source of it mattered not. He would not leave his position without answers.

When she leaned forward to peer past him, Conrad caught the faint scent of roses. It struck him that this was, in fact, the closest he had ever been to her.

"I would invite you inside—"

He did not hesitate. Moving past her, careful not to touch her, Conrad entered the chamber, only to freeze as he took in their surroundings. He'd almost forgotten.

He turned as the door scraped closed.

"Is it me who startles you so?" she asked, her eyes wide.

"Nay, 'tis this chamber." He did not elaborate.

"The Conrad I remember was not unsettled by anyone. Or anything."

How wrong she was.

Cait lifted her chin. "This was hers, wasn't it?" she asked.

In one of the many missives they'd exchanged since the tournament, Conrad had admitted he'd avoided the chambers used by his parents after their death. The lord and lady's chambers, the lord's solar, the gardens.

"How did you know?"

She didn't answer at first.

"'Tis close to the great hall, and more ornate than one might expect for a guest."

Every time Cait opened her mouth to speak, he was reminded of the impropriety of this discussion. He imagined closing the distance between them, pulling the only woman he'd ever loved into his arms, and making her his.

This very night.

But Conrad had given up on that dream years earlier.

When she'd abruptly stopped writing him.

"Why, Cait?"

Though he could reach her in two long strides, Conrad did not dare move. He needed her answer like he needed air. The not knowing had been so much worse than waiting for word from Dromsley.

Her letters had brought him more joy than winning his first joust or being named Earl of Licheford. They had partially healed his broken soul when both of his parents had died within a sennight of each other. They had helped soothe his bitter, angry heart after the king turned his back on Conrad's father—a man who'd always served the crown faithfully.

As always, bile rose in his throat when he thought of King John's response to his parents' simple request. Would it have made a difference if he'd intervened? Terric tended to believe not, but then, they would never know. John had refused. His only consolation was that he'd seen his parents one last time before they'd succumbed to the illness that had spread through Licheford like fire through a field of straw.

He had told Cait as much in a letter, and her response had done much to allay his anger.

She sighed, grasping her hands in front of her. "There is much I wish to say."

Conrad waited. He wanted nothing more than that explanation, and now that she stood before him, ready to give it, his chest constricted with the anticipation.

Cait. Here at Licheford.

Did this mean . . .

"After that day, hatred consumed Terric. It didn't matter to him that the man who'd attempted to hurt me was dead. He hated him, and he blamed the king for choosing his companions so poorly. He blames John by association!"

"I know it well. But that hardly explains why you stopped writing me."

"All that hatred changed him."

Her delicate shoulders rose and fell, the wood crackling behind them making Conrad well aware of their location—and what would happen should anyone find them here. Neither of them dared to move. To sit. To relax for even a moment.

"He blamed himself, though I often reminded him that I was not harmed."

Conrad shook off the thought of that man on top of her, his hand under her gown. He'd kill him again, if given the chance.

"So many times I tried to tell him. To explain the truth."

"Cait, do not say it." He knew what was coming.

"It was my fault. It was my idea to meet you along that river. You warned me it wasn't safe, but I still insisted, and you were forced to kill that man because of me."

"You cannot still believe that." But he could tell she did. Even before the words left his mouth, Conrad knew she did blame herself. She always had. It wrenched what was left of his heart in two. Although he knew it wouldn't help, that Cait wouldn't believe him if he told her it wasn't her fault, something he'd told her many times, he couldn't stay silent. "You did not ask to be attacked."

Cait was not even listening to him. "You warned me," she continued, "said it was not safe."

He remained silent this time, gently shaking his head.

"He changed after that day."

"And has become quite a man." He didn't dare say it, but he suspected Terric was better, stronger, because of what had happened.

"Why did you stop writing to me?" he asked again.

A knock at the door prevented Cait from answering.

"Cait?"

It was Terric's wife.

Another knock. "Cait, are you sleeping?"

They locked eyes once more, and then Conrad moved to the door.

"No!" she whispered fiercely, her tone frantic.

But he would not hide. If she'd come to England after all this time, there was a reason for it. He would learn that reason, but first they would stop hiding that they had been important to each other. They'd done enough of that.

"Conrad!"

Conrad glanced at her over his shoulder, not bothering to mask his confusion and pain, then reached the door and pulled it open.

"She is awake," he said to Lady Roysa, her rounded eyes no less than what he would have expected. "I was just leaving."

"Conrad, wait."

He wanted to stay. Part of him was still desperate for answers.

But the cynic inside him, born of pain and sorrow, insisted it did not matter. He wasn't the same man who'd been beguiled by a young Scottish lady at the tournament. Who had longed to learn more. Who had fallen in love with that very lady through her letters.

She was here, aye, but too much had passed between them.

CHAPTER 6

The members of the order had been locked
away all morning, but they were no closer to
an agreement about how to proceed than
when all four men had arrived in Conrad's south solar. All morning he and Terric had circled each other,
a natural extension of the more private conversation
they'd had prior to the meeting. When Terric had
pulled him aside to ask about Cait, Conrad had answered him directly, his tone unequivocal.

"'Tis your sister's story to tell. When she does, I'll
gladly speak of it."

The fact that Terric had accepted his stance,
though begrudgingly, told him Roysa had not informed her husband of Conrad's late-night visit.

They'd begun the meeting and soon reached this
stalemate—Conrad believed one course of action was
best, Terric and Lance disagreed.

"We have the authority to communicate directly
with the king," Conrad said again.

A midday meal had just been brought for them,
but none had touched it. Terric, the most vocal opponent to his plan, stood from his seat and moved toward the tray.

"We cannot wait. The others granted us the authority to act because they expect us to do so." He picked up a piece of dried meat. "I refuse to wait any longer."

"The waiting," Lance agreed, "is intolerable."

He, too, followed Terric to the tray of food, his blacksmith's arms flexing as he reached for a chunk of bread. Lance was now the lord of Tuleen, but Conrad could still see the boy he'd been. Brooding but steady, trustworthy to the core.

"I would not argue with you there." He leaned forward, setting his elbows on his knees. "We would need considerable support from within the city's gates. Taking London would not be a simple matter."

Guy rolled his eyes. "You mean to say we cannot stroll into the city and demand all those loyal to King John lay their weapons at our feet?"

Getting Guy to be serious apparently took more than a plot to overthrow the king. The man feared nothing. Although his friend's comment annoyed him, he knew better than to say so. It would only give way to another jest.

"We can try," he said instead, shooting Guy a look that his friend cheerfully ignored. Although Conrad's father had taught him to lead with nothing more than his eyes—such tactics didn't work on the mercenary. "In fact, I very much like your idea. Let us do it exactly like that."

"Very good, then. As it feels like action we must take."

At first Conrad thought his friend continued to jest, but Guy's tone gave him pause. He exchanged a glance with him to confirm it. This was more than a suggestion. The mercenary had a sense of things that could not be explained. Guy was telling him he had as much now. A fact Conrad would not ignore, no matter how unusual his premonitions may seem.

"You both need to eat," Terric said, popping another piece of meat into his mouth.

Nodding, Conrad stood and approached the platter.

"Roysa said your cook is a man," Terric commented, reaching for a mug of ale.

"Elizabeth died," he said flatly. "The king's evil."

Everyone in the room froze. They all gave him the same look, as if death from such an illness was particularly dreadful.

Conrad despised pity.

"But I thought . . . when?" Terric asked.

"Just last summer."

He knew what Terric was going to say. He'd thought Conrad's parents had been the last two to succumb to the illness that had claimed so many lives at Licheford.

"No others seemed to be inflicted this time," he said, refusing to think of his parents. "And thankfully, her wasting away was much more brief than the others."

Neither bloodletting nor purgatives did anything to improve her, or the other victims, and although one of the finest physicians in England had attended to her—to them—the treatment had been ineffective.

With mumbled apologies, the men ate. Conrad was sorry to have soured the mood, but he would not hesitate to use it to his advantage. They needed to provide a united front.

"The other barons have given us leave to act on their behalf. We move toward London."

The others were slow to respond. His tone brooked no argument, and none was given.

Terric looked at him for a moment, then said, "We

will need to send messages ahead to our allies within the city. Should we also shore up our foreign allegiances, specifically ties to France?"

"We will not all go to London at once, but aye, I believe we should do both."

"Are you suggesting we split up? In different directions?" Terric asked.

"I am," he said. "We'll cover more ground that way, and it'll make it more difficult for his people to find us all."

Conrad could see Lance and Guy considering it.

"Bishop Salerno must be informed at once," Lance said, naming one of the key supporters of their cause. Without allies in the Church, they had no chance. Keeping the bishop informed was essential. "I will go to him."

"Noreham." Guy grabbed his own mug of ale. "We will ready for London there and coordinate contact with those on the inside."

The possibility of taking the city, even though the king was not in residence, had been bandied about since the start of their rebellion. All twenty barons had agreed that seizing it would be the quickest path to gaining John's agreement to sign the Charter of Liberties, which would essentially blunt his power. But they'd hoped they would not need to take such a risk.

"I will take my men south, informing the others along the way as well as ensuring French support," he agreed.

"And I will bring my men all the way to the city walls. Send the message that we have the men necessary to take the city by force, if needed." Terric raised his chin, defying any of them to disagree. It was a dangerous proposition, for the only reason a northern border lord would have to be in such a place with a contingent of men was as an open provocation against King John.

The four men watched one another, each daring the others to voice a final concern. To stop the wheels of war they'd begun to turn.

But none did.

It was the logical next step, the path that needed to be taken.

CHAPTER 7

"Cait Kennaugh."

Her shoulders sagged at the sound of her brother's voice behind her. Cait tried to smile but could tell from Roysa's face her efforts failed. She'd been relieved when the men hadn't joined them for the midday meal. It had felt like a welcome respite—which had now come to an end.

"I would like to speak to my sister, if it pleases you."

That must have been for the benefit of Roysa, who'd followed Cait out of the great hall, trying to encourage her to go for a walk, a ride, something. What Roysa really wanted was an explanation, she knew. Now she'd have to give one to her brother instead. Roysa shot her a look that clearly indicated she'd stay if Cait wanted her to. Part of her wanted to accept the offer, but it would only be a temporary reprieve. Cait nodded slightly, and Roysa gave her one last look before walking away.

It was time to confess.

She'd thought about doing so many times. But she and Conrad had stopped corresponding, and it had no longer seemed so pressing.

Until her mother had forced her to make a decision about Colin MacGregor. Marry him or else explain why not. He was the son of their closest ally and neighbor. A kind, handsome man any woman would be honored to take as a husband.

But he was not Conrad.

And so she'd fled.

Leaving her mother a note of explanation, she'd followed Rory for as long as possible without being noticed. He'd tried to send her back, of course, but she'd refused, and he'd relented. And now she was here.

"You wish to speak to me?" she said with a smile.

Terric had a weakness for smiles. Always had, even as a child. Although hers seemed more effective than most, until Roysa of course.

He pulled her into an alcove with nothing to recommend it. Just a curved stone wall, an arrowslit, and a semiprivate place to speak.

"Your smile will not soften me."

Ah, but it would. Her brothers could intimidate her on the training field, where their raw strength was on display, but not here. Not in alcoves or drawing rooms.

"I do love you for caring," she said honestly. "And for protecting me, always."

Still grimacing, though not as deeply, Terric crossed his arms.

Cait took a deep breath to steady herself. Sharing did not come naturally for her. Perhaps it had, at one time. Cait could not recall. But certainly it did not now.

"It began quite by accident," she said at last. "We sat together, you and I, breaking our fast, when Bailey was summoned."

Terric's brows drew together. Apparently he

hadn't expected the discussion would turn to Bradon Moor's longtime messenger.

"You gave him a missive, for Conrad. I wanted to add a brief note, but Rory interrupted before I could ask you."

"As Rory does." Finally, a smile from her brother.

"So I didn't ask you. I wrote my own note and gave it to Bailey."

Thankfully, her mother had thought learning to write was as valuable as learning to read.

"A note to Conrad," Terric said to himself than to her.

Another servant passed, this time with a tray of freshly baked bread. The kitchens must be located nearby. Cait had not seen much of the keep yet, aside from her chamber and the great hall.

"Aye. To thank him for"—Terric winced—"helping me."

Her brother had likely thought she would say "saving me." Even after all this time he had difficulty accepting that strangers, specifically Conrad, had come to her aid.

Cait did not know which of the boys had seen her first or precisely how it had happened. One moment she was using every bit of strength she possessed to attempt to forestall the wretched man's hand from running up her thigh, and the next Terric was attempting to push him off her. The man, much older and more powerful than her brother, had given him a backhand so powerful it had thrown him to the ground. Three others had rushed forward, one grabbing his hand, another with a sword raised.

Cait brushed aside the memory. She'd become quite adept at doing so.

"When he wrote back, I thought to tell you. But . . ."

Terric's eyes narrowed with suspicion, just as she'd known they would. *This* was why she'd kept their correspondence a secret for so long. She forced herself to finish her statement. "I did not."

Putting her face in her hands, Cait closed her eyes against her brother's accusatory glare.

A moment passed, and then she felt his large hand covering her small one. Her cheeks tingled, but Cait would not let herself cry. Not yet. There was still too much to tell.

Uncovering her face, she took Terric's hand and squeezed it.

"His message contained nothing but a courtesy reply. And that may have been the end of our correspondence."

That he continued to hold her hand gave Cait the strength to continue, to say it all at once.

"It was not. I responded, this time asking Bailey not to mention my addition to your missive. With each letter, the secret grew. Until I stopped writing. I pleaded with Conrad not to make mention of it."

"Why, Cait?" her brother asked, his tone an entreaty. "What did you believe I would say?"

Taking comfort in their connection, she told the truth. "I did not know. And for this reason, I could not risk telling you. If you had ordered me to stop writing to him—"

"I'd never have done so."

"Perhaps not. But if you had, for reasons I could not contemplate, I could not bear it. We only exchanged a few letters a year, but the joy of receiving his letters . . . those became the happiest moments of my life."

She let her words penetrate.

"You had your training. Your tournament. Rory," Cait said, willing him to understand.

"I had only . . ."

She nearly said *Conrad*. But it seemed too intimate a thing to admit.

"Bradon Moor is beautiful. And more important, 'tis safe. But it has little else to offer a young woman besides embroidery and prayer and waiting for a potential suitor I may or may not care for to come along and take me as a wife. To force me from my home and my family. So that I might continue to learn embroidery in another prison."

There. She had said it.

"You hate embroidery," Terric said finally. "Cait, if Bradon Moor feels like a prison, it is because you made it so. You could have come to another tourney with us. Rory and I asked many times. "If," Terric said slowly, "you were writing to Conrad, if you had an affinity for him, then why did you refuse to come with us?"

Her inability to form an answer to that very question was the very reason she had stopped writing to Conrad. "I . . . do not know."

Her brother released her hand, his gaze turning incredulous.

"You do not know?"

If she had, Cait would have explained it to Conrad many years earlier. She would have told him the truth of it last night.

"Did you think you would be attacked again? That I wouldn't be able to protect you?"

"A braw warrior like you? Nay, I did not think it."

Not precisely, at least. She had no doubt Terric could protect her, and yet there was a tiny part of her that never felt safe. Maybe it never would.

"You can commiserate with Conrad on this," she said quietly, "as he asked me the same question so many times I could no longer count."

"Is that why you stopped writing? Because you refused to meet him again and had no explanation for it?"

"Of sorts."

There was more. Much more. But Cait could never tell him that part. She cared too much for his opinion of her.

"But you're here now. Why?"

This, at least, was easy.

"Mother insisted on knowing why I would not marry Colin MacGregor."

"I would have that answer too," a deep voice boomed from just around the bend of the alcove. Cait closed her eyes.

"And a few others, as well," Conrad said, coming into view just as her eyes popped open.

Her chest constricted as the two longtime friends stared at each other, her revelations having opened a rift between them. She knew that and hated herself a little for it. If Cait could go back to the beginning, that first moment with Bailey, she would tell him everything. Maybe even why she did not deserve Conrad's affection.

But she could not go back.

Neither could she hide now from either man, for it had been her idea to come here. She'd insisted on it. Channeling Roysa, Cait straightened her back, lifted her chin, and refused to apologize for that which she could not alter.

"'Tis good fortune you're here," she said to Conrad, noting that his dress was more formal than it had been the day before. He looked every bit the English earl, his surcoat emblazoned with the Licheford coat of arms, a black eagle on a field of gold. As tall as her brother, if not more so, his wide shoulders seemed to fill the alcove as his eyes bored into her. "I would have a word?"

She looked at Terric then, wishing she knew more of what he thought of her tale. But she and Conrad desperately needed to finish what they had started the evening before.

"Brother?"

She could have smiled. Tried to cajole him in that way. But Cait did not have a smile left in her. The knowledge that she had to bare herself to Conrad, explain that which she did not entirely understand, or this trip would be for naught . . . Cait simply could not do anything other than plead with her eyes for her brother to understand.

And he did.

Terric turned to Conrad. "I know you to be an honorable man, more than any other."

Conrad didn't respond.

"She is my sister."

Each of the four words was said with significance and emphasis, as if it held secret meaning.

"I know it well," Conrad answered with nearly as much brevity as Terric.

And then her brother slipped behind the wall, leaving them alone.

And while before the alcove seemed isolated, private, now Cait felt as exposed as if they were standing in the middle of the great hall.

When Conrad spoke, she nearly jumped backward at his abrupt tone. "Come with me."

CHAPTER 8

Conrad had already shared their plan with his marshal, a skilled swordsman who had led his father through more than one successful battle, but there was still much to be done before leaving. He would take nearly two hundred men, a large enough contingent to be of use if they could not peaceably overtake London.

But Conrad had no intention of leaving Licheford undefended either. He would keep his people, and Cait and others, safe.

Preparations needed to be made. There was work to be done. But this discussion could not wait.

He would not chance another interruption, hence their descent into the buttery.

"Conrad, where are we going?"

The air cooled as they wound their way down the stone stairwell.

"Careful," he said, turning. Though he'd thought to reach for a candle just before entering the dark space, it provided little light for him, less so for Cait, who followed.

If she were any other woman, he'd reach for her. But this was Cait. And she was not any other woman.

"The buttery," he said, holding the candle closer to her. "Can you see?"

"Aye."

She stepped into the room with him, and Conrad immediately went to work. Reaching for a wooden box, he removed four additional candles, their stands in a separate box just beside it. Using his own light, he lit all of them, placing them on top of four wine casks, illuminating the brightly colored stone walls around them.

Like any buttery for a castle such as Licheford, this chamber was as ornate as the one above it, a showcase of his great-grandfather's accumulated wealth. In some ways, this was the most important room in the keep, and it showed with bright colors and painted walls.

"'Tis beautiful."

Cait spun around, her cream and pale yellow gown gleaming against the flickering candlelight. He watched as errant strands of her hair kissed the bare shoulders that peeked out from what was a fairly modest gown for a woman of her status.

"It was long when I last saw you," he said of her hair.

The day after the attack. Terric and his brother had left before the tournament was over. He'd wanted desperately to say more to her that day. To ask if she was well. If she would return the following year. Instead, he had watched silently as the Kennaugh clan departed.

Although the other boys, Terric and Lance and Guy, who had been strangers to them at the time, had seen Cait and her attacker at the same time Conrad did, it was Conrad's sword that had pierced the man's heart. The blade had broken, and they'd dumped it into the river with the body.

"It's been short for many years."

As before, they stood too close. His body responded to the swell of her breasts, so he took a step back, hoping Cait did not notice.

"Colin MacGregor likes it short?"

He shouldn't be surprised that he'd made her wince. They had learned about each other through letters, and she had never borne the brunt of the ire that sometimes took hold and threatened to strangle him.

The legendary Licheford temper.

But he would not take the bitter words back. Conrad wanted her answer, to that and many other questions.

"Enough to wish to wed me," she shot back.

His jaw clenched.

"Who is he?"

He would not pretend that he didn't care. He would be leaving in two short days and had little time for flowery words.

"The son of a neighboring clan chief. A good man whom I've no reason not to marry."

No reason . . .

He forced his expression to remain neutral.

"But you told Terric you would not marry him. That you came here instead. Why, precisely?" Once he started talking, Conrad could not seem to stop. "Just as importantly, why did you stop writing? Do you know how many letters I sent after your last one?"

Despite knowing he should calm himself, Conrad could not.

"You asked me to keep our exchange from Terric, so I did. Despite all we've been through, your brother and I . . . despite the fact that he trusts me with his life, and I trust him with mine, not once did I tell him I'd confessed my love to his sister. A woman who glimpsed inside my very soul. Before she *crushed* it."

As he spoke, Conrad realized from the flicker in her eyes that she'd never even read those letters. The ones he continued to send after she ceased to respond.

"I wanted to read them. Broke every seal myself but . . ."

He could not do this. There was too much pain he had long ago buried.

Conrad tried to move past her, but Cait's gentle touch on his arm froze him in place as easily as the tip of a broadsword.

"Please."

Two layers of clothing separated him from her hand, but its featherlight touch penetrated them easily. It branded him.

"I cannot," he said, though Conrad did not move.

"You said you loved me."

"Once."

He continued walking, with difficulty, but did not ascend the stairs. He'd come to hear this, and so he would. No matter how difficult it might be. Turning toward her, Conrad hardened himself against her words, waiting for Cait to continue.

"I loved you too."

"No." He shook his head. "You did not. You stopped writing me, Cait. You never came."

Letter after letter, he'd begged her to return to the tournament.

They'd opened themselves to each other in a way people rarely did in person. Maybe because it was easier to write hard truths than it was to say them, or maybe because their connection had immediately been strong. Either way, he'd told her things he hadn't disclosed to anyone, and she had done the same.

They knew each other in a deep way that transcended the few times they'd seen each other in person.

He knew that she felt weak after the attack. That she'd despised her inability to fight back.

Conrad had encouraged her to speak to Terric, to ask him to train her too. But she'd said her brothers were much too stubborn—they'd consider it a slight on their ability to protect her.

He also knew that Cait saw everything. Observed everyone. Some thought her haughty because of it. Others believed her shy. But she was simply thoughtful, watching and waiting for the moment when her words would have an impact.

But for all he knew about this woman, there was so much he didn't understand, including why she had refused to meet him again in person. Once, Conrad had even suggested that he visit her at Bradon Moor.

It was the last time he'd ever heard from her.

"I am here now."

Their eyes locked.

Her meaning was clear.

When he'd overheard her speaking to Terric of Colin MacGregor . . . Conrad had not known what to think. Only that he needed to know if she had come here, to England, for him.

He had his answer.

"Why now? Why after all this time?"

"Colin—"

"Why now?" he repeated, angered at her poor timing. Angry, still, that she had allowed his heart to soar with hope, only to send it crashing down. Conrad did not know that he was capable of loving again, even her.

Some might say he had never *truly* loved her in the first place. A woman he'd never touched. Never kissed. But he knew otherwise.

Cait didn't answer. Maybe she didn't know the answer, but that simply was not good enough for him.

"I have to go."

This time, Conrad did not turn back. Heart hammering in his chest, he chided himself for thinking he would get answers from a woman so private her own brother had not known she'd fallen in love with his friend. With the man who bore the scar that reminded him of her every day of his life.

Cait Kennaugh was here.

For him.

Unfortunately, he could not be here for her.

CHAPTER 9

Sabine walked into the hall like a woman who had never once doubted herself, head held high, auburn hair flowing in every direction. Her husband must have done something to upset her because she swatted his hand away as they wound their way toward the head table for the evening meal.

"Well met, Guy," Terric said from his position on the other side of Roysa. Cait sat beside her too, with two empty seats on her left. She imagined they were for the couple who strode into the hall now, attracting attention from everyone, including her. "How is it possible someone so lovely would willingly marry *you?*"

Cait tried to smile but could not. Although she hadn't looked at Conrad directly since taking a seat, she was conscious of him all the same. After their failed talk, he'd disappeared for the remainder of the day. Cait had spent the afternoon with Roysa and Idalia, getting a tour of Licheford Castle and the grounds. Her sister-in-law had also relayed the distressing news that Conrad had failed to mention earlier, that the men would be leaving in two days. Cait had hardly spoken since then. Both Roysa and Idalia had asked, of course, if she were well.

Nay, she was not well at all.

Conrad was leaving, and they'd barely had a chance to speak. If their conversation in the buttery were any indication, coming here had been a mistake. He was unlikely to forgive her. But she refused to accept defeat just yet. She would get him alone again.

"Apologies, Lady Cait," Sabine said, sitting next to her. "We've hardly had an opportunity to speak since you arrived."

Cait didn't know what to say, so she blurted out the truth.

"You are very beautiful."

Had she really just said such a thing to a perfect stranger?

"Not so much as you, to be sure." Sabine leaned toward her. "I'm told you forced your brother Rory to take you to England with him, just as Dromsley Castle was under attack?"

She seemed mesmerized by the idea, so Cait hated to dissuade her. But that was not quite true.

"I did follow Rory, against my mother's orders, but I didn't know how much danger lay ahead. My brothers tell me little."

She picked up her goblet of wine, the noise from the hall increasing as retainers and servants filled it to near capacity.

"Good," Sabine said, seemingly satisfied.

Cait stared at her in confusion, but Sabine leaned over to address Roysa.

"Two of four?" she asked, winking to her.

Roysa frowned. "Aye. Two of four. He still says no," she whispered, looking back to see if her husband had heard. Terric seemed to be intent on his stew, though he did appear suspicious of Roysa's glance.

Sabine made a sound of disgust in her throat.

Cait looked back and forth between the women. "Two of four?"

Sabine glanced at her husband, and when she did, Cait could not help but follow her gaze—right past Guy and down to Conrad.

Damned if he wasn't looking directly at her.

She nearly smiled at the thought of how Terric or Rory would react to her silent sentiment, even though she'd not used the word aloud. Her brothers could swear, bed women, and risk their lives in battle. But if she dared to say "damn" or used any other such words, her brothers would immediately threaten to tell her mother.

And if there was one thing Mother did not tolerate, it was language that did nothing but "put your ignorance on display." Thankfully, it was the one instance in which she did not discriminate between Cait and her brothers. On more than one occasion, Cait had gotten them into trouble for their own bad language. Oh, how much fun they'd had.

Another memory, one of words Conrad had written, suddenly came to her.

They look to me to replace both of them, Father and Mother. I fear no one, including myself, could possibly be both. Some days the expectations of an entire earldom weigh heavy.

It had been three years since he'd written those words. The Conrad she watched now bore no resemblance to the one who worried about his ability to lead Licheford. This man led a country.

Cait tore her gaze from him, chastising herself for being a fool. For thinking he could forgive her for having abandoned him.

"Lady Cait?"

She'd hoped Sabine wouldn't notice her silent regard.

"Cait, please," she said, taking a bite of stew. "I am a fool."

"Nay," Sabine whispered back.

Cait hadn't realized she'd said the words aloud.

"We've not had an opportunity to speak much." Sabine placed her wine goblet onto the table, a single drop of red dripping onto the white linen below. "But I know."

Although Sabine was a virtual stranger, the words didn't surprise her. These men, her brother and the others, were as much brothers as Terric and Rory. Their wives, it appeared, had forged the same type of bond.

Suddenly, she wanted to be a part of that nearly as much as she wanted Conrad back in her life.

"Lady Sabine—"

"My given name, if you please."

Cait glanced toward the center of the table, but Conrad was no longer watching them.

"I am not sorry you know some of what is between us. But there is more. Much more. And I *am* a fool," she said with conviction.

Sabine leaned so close a faint scent of roses drifted toward her.

"I know more than you realize. I've wintered here, you see. I have grown quite close to Conrad."

Sitting up, Sabine lifted her wooden spoon and began to eat. As if she'd not just given Cait a clue to the puzzle that was the earl.

She waited for the mercenary's wife to say more, but she did not seem inclined to do so. Instead, Cait ate in silence as Sabine spoke animatedly to her husband. He teased her mercilessly, and Sabine teased back. Neither stopped smiling for the duration of the meal, and it was only as dessert was served that Cait remembered the odd comment from earlier.

"Two of four?" she asked as Sabine licked a bit of tart from her lip. "What does that mean?"

"'Tis just us remaining. We still need to convince them," Roysa answered beside her.

Cait had not realized she'd spoken loudly enough to be overhead.

"Convince whom? Of what?"

Suddenly looking quite guilty, Roysa glanced at Terric, who was looking at something near the hall's entrance, then leaned toward her.

"That we will not be staying at Licheford when they leave."

Terric leaned forward, touching Roysa's arm. In an admirable effort to distract him, Roysa lifted her goblet for a toast.

Cait could not be more confused.

We will not be staying at Licheford. 'Tis just us remaining.

She thought back to their earlier conversation, working out the details. So the women did not wish to remain here as their husbands left for the south. Sabine and Idalia had convinced their husbands already, which left just Roysa and . . .

Her eyes flew to Sabine's.

The men were not traveling together. She knew that much from Roysa. Each had a mission, all ending outside the gates of London, where they would meet in a final bid to force the king's hand.

In preparation to possibly take over the greatest city in England.

And the ladies were joining them. All but Roysa and . . . "Surely she does not mean . . . ?"

But Sabine was already nodding her head. Apparently Guy and Conrad were the only two remaining who still needed to be convinced to take a companion to London.

"I cannot. He does not want me," she stopped. Sabine's smile wasn't meant to pacify—it was a knowing smile. As if she did, indeed, know something about Conrad and Cait. As if she expected him to take her to London, which was a ridiculous notion given the state of their relationship. Not to mention the fact that Terric would never, ever allow it.

"Nay." Cait reached for her wine and took a sip. "Nay, I will not . . . he will not . . ."

"Trust me," Sabine said, but her gaze fixed on something, or rather someone, in the hall, and her smile suddenly faltered. Roysa followed her gaze to a woman watching them closely. The woman was sitting, but it did nothing to hide her voluptuous figure in her deep green velvet gown. Long blonde hair streamed behind her, a simple headdress hiding nothing. She was so very different from Cait, in all ways but one way.

The way she looked at Conrad . . .

Before she could stop herself, Cait confirmed her suspicion by looking at Sabine . . . and then Conrad. He wasn't looking at the woman now, but Cait could be patient. Surely he would eventually notice her staring at him with unbridled desire.

"Cait," Sabine said, interrupting her musings. "She means nothing to him."

Cait continued her vigil. Finally, he noticed. But she did not know Conrad well enough to discern the look he gave the blonde woman.

You know him better than most.

That may have been true once, but no longer.

"Who is she?"

Sabine sighed.

"Who is she?" she repeated, unable to look away.

"Lady Threston," Sabine finally answered. Though really it was no answer at all.

"Please, Sabine. Who is she?"

Still, Sabine did not answer. She nodded instead, confirming her suspicions.

Conrad's paramour. Unless . . .

Heart in her throat, she asked, "Are they betrothed?"

She'd forgotten to whisper. Guy leaned forward, hearing her.

"Nay, my lady, they are not."

He and Sabine exchanged a look that told Cait she, and perhaps Lady Threston, had been a topic of discussion between them.

Her only consolation? Both of them seemed to be on her side. But that hardly mattered. There was only one side that did, and it was the man who finally seemed to realize what they were all talking about.

Conrad looked from his lady back to her, but again she could not read anything into his expression. Cait pretended it was nothing. She picked up the last tart in front of her and took a bite, forcing it down her throat. It stuck in her chest, heavy and unwanted, but she forced another, chiding herself for thinking Conrad would be alone. A man such as he? A handsome earl?

Of course there would be other women.

Sabine had it wrong.

She *was* a fool and should never have come.

CHAPTER 10

"She refuses to listen," Sabine said to Roysa, ignoring Cait altogether, a tricky business given she was sitting right beside her. In Cait's bedchamber, no less.

A full day had passed since she had learned of Lady Threston. Since the others had begun their campaign to persuade Cait to appeal to Conrad. And while the thought of accompanying him on the dangerous journey south, with men equally as dangerous, excited her as much as it did the others, she simply would not do it. Not after the buttery. Not after realizing there was a woman in Conrad's life.

"You are married. All of you," she said to the women gathered in her bedchamber. By rights all four of them should be sleeping. Instead, they prepared to ride out on the morrow.

All except for her.

"I am nothing to Conrad."

Sabine threw up her hands. "As I've said since yesterday, that is simply not true."

"Listen to her," Idalia cut in. By far the quietest of the four, she had a determined manner that made people listen when she talked. "Sabine and Conrad have become close."

"When I first came to Licheford"—Sabine leaned forward on the padded bench that she and Cait shared—"and Conrad and I learned we had both lost our parents suddenly, his to illness and mine . . ."

Sabine shook her head as if ridding herself of a wretched memory.

"His mother made many of the tapestries in the hall."

"I know," Cait whispered. According to Conrad, it had been her greatest joy—she'd loved weaving bright colors into stories for all to enjoy.

"My mother, though not by trade, was a master girdler."

Cait was happy they'd been able to comfort each other. She too knew the pain of losing a parent and could not imagine if her mother had been taken from them too.

"I am so very sorry," she said, though Sabine hardly seemed to hear her.

"When he looks at you—" Sabine waited until all eyes were on her to continue. "When he looks at you, I've no doubt there is more than any of us under-stands about your connection."

That, at least, was true.

Because he had saved her? Because he bore the scar to prove it? Or had that come later, after their years of exchanged letters?

She wanted to ask the questions aloud. Instead, Cait closed her eyes and bent her head down. "If he felt something once, I've ruined it."

"Nay," Sabine said gently. "Damaged, not ruined."

She kept her eyes closed. It was easier for her to speak this way, to face their silent judgement.

"After the tournament, we wrote to each other."

That part was easy enough. "I thanked him. I never told Terric, but it continued for many years. Until . . ."

Opening her eyes, she held back the tears that had gathered there, traitors to the story she told herself over and over and over again—that she had no place in this English earl's life. That he was a better man for not being reminded of the scar he bore.

"Until I stopped."

There. She had said it. And waited for the inevitable.

"Why?"

It was Idalia who'd asked. And as usual, Cait had no answer. They all were trying so hard to help her. Would they stop if they knew everything?

"He'd become more persistent. Asking for me to return to England, with Terric."

Cait shook her head.

Say it. Tell them. Just say it.

"Why did you not return?"

The gentleness and concern in Roysa's voice was the catalyst that finally sent the tears tumbling down her cheeks. The others didn't hesitate—Sabine put her arm around her, Roysa knelt at her feet, Idalia huddled next to her.

She was surrounded by sympathy. Actually surrounded, and Cait had no choice. Her tears came quicker, sobs shaking her shoulders as a handkerchief was shoved into her hands. She covered her face with it, remembering.

Oh God, I am so very sorry, Conrad. Terric. Guy. Lance.

What they'd been forced to do.

For *her.*

"It was my fault." Was that even her voice?

"Terric," she managed. "And Rory. They were always around. Always so protective."

Cait had caught the eye of the handsome earl's son, and in a wild moment of thoughtlessness, she'd asked for Conrad to meet her, alone.

"I told him to meet me by the river. Behind the tents."

She could see his face, less hardened than it was now but every bit as strong. "He refused, said it was not safe."

What a silly girl she had been, thinking she was actually a woman. Her very first time away from Bradon Moor. What had she known?

Nothing.

"I pleaded, like a silly girl." She opened her eyes. "Just one brief moment alone." She made a sound. "I'd dreamt of a kiss, and got much more in the bargain."

"No," Roysa said, her voice firm. "This was *not* your fault, Cait. No."

She ignored the words. "He said, ''Tis too dangerous,' but I went anyway. By the time he realized it . . ."

When had her tears stopped?

"I wanted to tell the others. To tell my brother. So many times, I tried. Started to say the words, to apologize."

"Listen to us." Roysa grabbed her hand, sitting next to her. "You've naught to apologize for. What young woman would not want to steal a kiss from a man such as Conrad? Silly girl? Nay, you were all of us. Do not think that way any longer."

The others nodded in agreement, and Cait was surprised to find herself smiling. A small smile but a genuine one.

"I stole a kiss from Lance well before it was proper. Each of us"—Idalia nodded to the others —"has a similar tale. Fortunately, none of us were accosted by a despicable man too drunk on his own self-importance and power to respect a young woman. 'Twas his fault, and he paid dearly for it. As befitted him."

"I never told Terric," she repeated.

"A fact that does not matter," Roysa said. "It does not matter why you were out there that day. What happened brought them together."

"They killed a man because of me."

"A man," Sabine said, squeezing her shoulders, "who tried to rape a young girl. Who attempted to kill four boys audacious enough to prevent him from committing the worst sort of injustice."

Cait tried again. "But don't you see? I never told him." She turned to Roysa. "Terric. He does not know. I . . . I couldn't . . ."

"He will not learn of it from me." She raised her chin. "The men made a pact that day, and we will make her own."

A chill ran through Cait, though not an entirely unpleasant one.

"All four of us will go to London. We will persevere against a corrupt king and return here, to Licheford, for a wedding."

"All four? Roysa, you are mistaken." The wedding was so outrageous a notion, she didn't even feel the need to address it.

"You *will* go with Conrad," Sabine agreed as if the matter were settled.

"He will not take me."

Roysa frowned, standing. "Did Rory 'take' you?"

She blinked, finally understanding.

"He will send me back," she argued. But it seemed none of the women were listening to her. "He hates me for abandoning him," she insisted.

Sabine pulled her to her feet, the others looking at her as if they were in on a secret she had yet to learn.

"He does not hate you, Cait. He loves you. And

once he realizes you only stopped writing him because you thought to punish yourself for something that was never your fault . . . he will understand. You will make him understand."

You thought to punish yourself for something that was never your fault.

"But it is, was, my . . ."

She stopped when all three women glared at her, looking at her with fire in their eyes, with a determination that Cait neither understood nor felt. But the idea of denying them was even more terrifying than following Conrad to London.

More terrifying than what he would do when he realized she'd defied him.

More terrifying than confessing that she'd not stopped thinking of him, not for one day, since that tournament.

CHAPTER 11

"Refuses to come out?"

He tried to do what Sabine had suggested, but deep breathing did not help. Not this time. He could feel the familiar creeping of heat up his neck.

He'd wondered why she hadn't answered in response to his knocking this morning, but he hadn't expected this. He hadn't thought she'd simply ignore him. That she'd refuse to say goodbye. Now he stood in the great hall, pacing. His pulse like a rabbit's. He'd thought he would at least see her one more time . . .

"Conrad," Guy said, using a tone no one else would dare take with him. "Your men are waiting."

He looked from the mercenary to his wife. They were ready, all of them, to leave Licheford and begin the next part of this dangerous adventure. He and Terric would leave this morn, since their voyages would take longer, and Guy and Lance would depart on the morrow. They'd meet outside of London around the same time.

The plan was set. The courtyard was filled with men and supplies. All was at the ready, except . . . he could not leave. Not like this.

Not without saying goodbye.

"I am sorry," Sabine said, just as she had the evening before when Cait had not come down to the evening meal. Despite promising himself he would not do so, Conrad had gone to her, only to find an empty chamber. The condition of the bed covers and the way the chairs were turned about made it look as if the other ladies had gathered there earlier.

While he should have been thinking of their plans, ensuring all was ready, Conrad had lain awake wondering why Cait had come all this way if simply to avoid him. The same question assailed him now.

Well, it would have to remain another mystery. There was much to be done, and he could no longer concern himself with the whims of a woman who clearly did not want to be found. It seemed to be Cait's specialty.

Guy and Sabine sat to break their fast, but Conrad kept up his pacing, nearly running into Terric. He immediately asked him the very question he'd promised himself he would not ask.

"Have you spoken to your sister?"

His friend gave him a look that made him immediately regret having spoken.

"You're angry," he said, not for the first time since the group had arrived in Licheford.

Terric shot a glance at the table, where Lance and Idalia had joined Guy and Sabine, then ushered Conrad to the side of the hall.

"Understandably so," Conrad continued. "But we leave today to force the hand of a king."

Terric crossed his arms, unimpressed with the seriousness of their circumstances. "You corresponded with my sister. For years. And never thought to make mention of it?"

Conrad clenched his jaw—he knew he deserved

that, and in truth, he had no real response. Of course he had thought to make mention of it. Many, many times. But Cait had begged him not to do so. A fact he would let her share with her brother, if she had not done so already.

It was not his place to say anything.

"You should speak to Cait about that."

Terric threw up his hands. "If she'd not bolted herself inside her bedchamber, I'd have done so. She tells me little, yet she risked her life to be here. Why, Conrad? Why now? I know you spoke with her, at least once."

Conrad caught his marshal's eye from across the hall. The man made a gesture indicating it was time. Nodding, he turned his attention back to Terric.

"The men are ready."

Terric didn't move.

He sighed. "I spoke to her, but we resolved nothing."

"Do you love her?"

It was the one question he hadn't expected. How much had Cait told him? He decided he would be as honest as possible without betraying her confidence.

"I did, once."

"But no longer?"

Roysa walked up to them then, cloaked. He still could not believe all three women were traveling south. Actually, Sabine's participation made sense. She bore the mark of the order, the fleur-de-lis on her back similar to their own marks. Her parents had taken a stand against King John long before Conrad and the others had formed the order. She deserved to see their mission through, despite the danger.

But Idalia and Roysa . . . this would be dangerous for them. Although he didn't doubt Terric's and Lance's ability to keep them safe, he wouldn't want his own wife anywhere near London. Of course, he had no wife. Nor was it his decision.

"She still will not come?" Conrad asked, Roysa's presence allowing him to avoid his friend's question.

Why did Roysa avoid her husband's gaze? And his own?

"Nay. Perhaps we should leave. The courtyard is filled with men . . ."

He watched her carefully. When Terric leaned down to place a kiss on his wife's cheek, a flush crept up her cheeks. She seemed almost . . . guilty. Something was amiss, but Conrad had no notion of what it could be, and Terric didn't seem to notice.

"Shall we go?"

When Roysa nodded, Terric extended his hand to Conrad.

Conrad clasped it, harder than was his custom. Although the Scot hadn't said so, his gesture made it clear that, although he was displeased, their friendship remained intact. Dented, perhaps. But not broken as Conrad had once feared.

"She will be safe here," he reassured Terric, and himself.

Conrad had decided to take just over fifty men. Much less than they'd originally intended, but all four of them, including his marshal, had agreed. If it became necessary to take London by force, they would send for reinforcements. With King John in Battleboro, his forces could be mobilized sooner than the king's.

Still so much uncertainty. But such was the case in a rebellion.

Releasing Terric's hand, Conrad followed him and Roysa from the hall after saying goodbye to the others, looking back one last time. Though he did not expect to see her, he was still oddly disappointed when there was no sign of Cait.

The noise of his men, and Terric's, reached them before they even stepped out of the keep. Although their retinue was modest, horses of all kinds—sumpters and ponies, and the destriers that would be needed in case of battle—mingled with squires and pages as they finished loading the supply carts.

Conrad spotted the fisherman who would assist in feeding them between lodgings and his own squire, Christopher, loading Conrad's personal packhorse. The day was cool, and Christopher handed him a thick mantle as he approached his mount.

"Ansel will ride at the front, my lord."

Ansel being his marshal.

Conrad glared at the boy of ten and five, the marshal's own son. The boy had likely saved Conrad's life at the last Tournament of the North. Christopher had insisted on repairing the stop-rib of his left cuisse, despite his protests that the repair was unnecessary and too time-consuming. Later, of course, his opponent's lance grazed that very thigh. The armor had protected his groin as designed, and he'd thanked the boy, who had beamed for days, telling the tale to all who would listen.

"Tell Ansel—"

"I cannot, my lord," the boy said, his cheeks slightly red. "He knew you would protest and has already ridden out."

"Ridden out?" Conrad boomed. He'd just seen the man moments earlier in the hall. "He cannot . . ."

Taking a deep breath, he thought about his wayward marshal, deliberately disobeying his orders. Conrad's father had always ridden at the front, and he'd taken up the practice despite protestations from Ansel and the captain of his guard.

"He will hear about it this eve," he grumbled.

Terric and Roysa had already moved away, surrounded by their clansmen and the knights of Dromsley who had accompanied him.

Upon closer inspection, Conrad should have known Ansel had left already with some of the men. Just half of their number remained, waiting on him. Conrad could catch him, ride to the front, and send the marshal back. But he didn't want to shame the man or lead the men to question his authority. And so he swallowed his anger and mounted, indicating that Christopher should do the same.

Gripping the reins, he gave the command and the entire courtyard of knights, soldiers, and servants began to advance. Turning one last time, he looked toward the direction of Cait's bedchamber, even though he knew he'd not see her through the narrow arrowslits in the stone.

He could not think of her now. She'd refused to say goodbye, even knowing he may never return. Even knowing he might *die*. That he'd allowed himself to be surprised, again, said more about him than it did Cait. Still, after all this time, he had been willing to talk again. To try to understand.

You are a Goddamn fool, Conrad.

He turned back, gripped his horse with his legs, and spurred it forward.

Their journey had begun.

CHAPTER 12

I f she had thought the journey from Bradon
Moor to Dromsley difficult, this one was much
more so. It was warmer, aye, and the sun had
been out for most of the day. But she and the other
ladies had not accounted for the pronounced dearth
of women in Conrad's retinue.

Still, she had not yet been noticed among the servants, not even when she snuck off during their
midday rest to relieve herself. It had been only one of
many narrow escapes that day.

She could ride as easily as the men. Her brothers
had ensured that, Rory being an expert horseman,
even more so than Terric. The hose and surcoat she
wore as a disguise were much preferable to a riding
gown, so comfort was not a concern.

Keeping her hood raised and her mouth shut,
however, was more difficult. She'd had to ignore
every order or question thrown her way, and "sim-
pleton" was the nicest of the epithets that had been
tossed her way.

Conrad's men, it turned out, used quite colorful
language when not in the company of women.

According to Roysa, who had learned of Conrad's

plan from Terric, they would camp along the road this night before arriving at Valence Castle the following eve. Once they did stop, she would reveal herself. It was the moment she'd been dreading, and wishing for, all day.

How would Conrad react? Would she be able to convince him to let her stay?

Finally, it happened. Conrad yelled for the men to halt and their party stopped for the night.

Cait tied off her mare, disappeared once more into the thick woods, and hid her belongings before joining the others. Sitting back from the fire now, she waited for the right moment. She only hoped it would not throw Conrad into a fit of anger.

His father had indulged in them quite often. Conrad did not, but it was a constant battle.

Cait nibbled on the provisions Idalia had secured just for her, the hard bread a welcome refreshment. As more and more men joined the one large fire in the center of camp, she thought back to one of Conrad's letters, the contents of which she had long since memorized.

By God's body, you will not hang my nephew. You'll see two hundred lanced knights on your land before you hang him!" Those were the words my father once spoke against the king, and this, while he was still one of his advisors. Later, when King Henry put the case up for trial, my father appeared in court with two hundred knights, just as he'd promised. A bold move, even for an earl. But my cousin did not hang. And I think the king respected him more for it, for a time at least.

Ofttimes I wish to be as cool and collected as your brother, but others, when I see spittle coming from my father's mouth in a fit of rage, I wish to inherit that fire but perhaps without the brimstone.

It was hard to imagine him angry, just now. He sat

casually atop a log between his squire and his marshal, the boy's father. She'd heard there was some disagreement between them earlier, but you would never know it at this moment.

They laughed as if they hadn't a care in the world. Conrad looked younger when he smiled, the white of his teeth evident even from this distance. His surcoat abandoned, his linen shirt rolled to his elbows, he looked more relaxed than he had since she'd arrived at Licheford.

Perhaps it was because he thought he'd left her behind . . .

"Move off, boy."

With a hard shove, Cait was pushed off the flat rock she'd found behind the rest of the camp. Before realizing she'd done so, Cait let out a sound, startled.

A very ladylike sound.

"Is that . . . are you . . . ?"

She had no time to react before her hood was tossed down. The churl who'd done it, and who had pushed her from the rock, looked as surprised as she felt.

A bushy auburn beard covered so much of his face, Cait focused on his eyes instead. Blue. Very blue. And extremely confused.

"A woman?"

She dared not look at Conrad. By now, the man's accusation had attracted the attention of the men closest to them. It would only be a matter of time before he came over. So be it. Cait had known she would be discovered before too long. The plan had always been to tell him before it was time to sleep. A woman alone among over fifty men? Nay, she wouldn't risk it.

With the crowd that had gathered around her, she

could not see him coming. But that voice was easily recognizable.

"What the devil?"

They parted to allow him a closer look.

At the woman. Disguised—poorly—as a boy. Idalia had braided her hair, but Cait had relied on the hood to keep her hidden. Without it, she was very much on display.

"Cait?"

Her small shrug was meant as an apology for deceiving him, for destroying the easy moment he had been enjoying with his marshal.

"Good eve, my lord."

"Good . . . ," Conrad sputtered, unmoving. "What are you . . . Cait, no."

She gave him a smile. "Aye."

He was not placated.

"You cannot . . . what are you doing here? Nay, don't tell me. It does not matter. You are going back."

She gestured to the night sky. "In the dark?"

He glared at the half moon as if it were King John himself.

"Come. With. Me."

She didn't move even when he turned from her. Even when she was gently pushed by one of Conrad's men.

"Now," he barked. And as much as she disliked orders, Cait followed this one. She couldn't stay outside with the men, after all, and it was unnecessary to make him even angrier. She tried to ignore the stares and whispers as she walked by.

His was the largest tent, large enough for him to stand inside. Pushing back the flap, he allowed it to close behind him, not bothering to keep it open for her. Oh, he was angry.

Cait took a deep breath, her hand on the flap.

This was precisely what she wanted, was it not? Conrad as a captive audience. A chance to explain, as best she could, and find out if coming to England had been as big a folly as it seemed.

Ignoring the snickers behind her, Cait opened the flap and stepped inside.

CHAPTER 13

Conrad didn't know if he wanted to shake Cait or kiss her.

In fact, he *did* know. He would do both if given the chance. To think the ladies had so deliberately misled him.

They'd been planning this. She'd been planning this, and now she was here. Opening his tent. Standing before him.

He would not look down. Nor would he notice the curve of her legs in those hose.

"You're angry."

Ah, God. Yes. No. He was confused as hell.

"Cait, do you realize the kind of danger you're in? Tomorrow morn you must go back. With two men. You cannot be here."

That look, the one she gave him now—it was one of the reasons she'd so attracted him at the tournament all those years ago. She'd had the same mixture of innocence and resolve, even then.

"The others have gone as well. With their husbands. You should let me stay."

Sabine. Idalia. Roysa.

Conrad shook his head. "I am not your husband." He waved his hands frantically around them. "You are alone. Unchaperoned. There's not one other woman to be found in this camp." He shook his head. "No, I cannot. We cannot. Terric will kill us both."

Cait rolled her eyes. "Terric will not kill you. 'Twas my choice to come. Mayhap you've not noticed, Conrad, but I'm not a young girl any longer. Terric is, in fact, my junior.

Though Terric was only younger than him by one year, Conrad and Cait the same age at nine and twenty, she spoke the truth. But that didn't mean his friend would not still kill him when next they met.

"I promised him," he ground out, unable to form a coherent thought.

Cait planted her hands on her slender hips. "You promised what, precisely? That you would not find yourself alone with me? That you would not do . . . what did you promise?"

"I promised to act honorably."

"This is not honorable? Us speaking? We are simply—"

He moved quickly.

Wrapping his hand behind her head, Conrad brought her lips to his. The shock of it took him aback—he'd intended to honor his word to Terric. And Cait clearly did not know how to react.

What to do.

He showed her. Gliding his tongue against the folds of her lips, he told her, without speaking, to open for him.

She did.

Slanting his head, he pulled her closer, touching his tongue to hers.

Cait immediately responded. Within a few moments, she understood completely. Her mouth moved effortlessly against his, and the sweetness she gave, Conrad willingly took.

When her hands settled tentatively on his forearms, her warm touch only served to inflame him. He should go gently, but Conrad had dreamed of this moment for what felt like his entire life.

She was not his.

She'd stopped writing.

Her brother would certainly kill him.

But this was *Cait*. She stood in his tent, looking at him as if he would save her from the confusion they both felt. And God help him, Conrad wanted to heal the breach between them. He wanted to be the man he'd once been, the one who had killed her attacker, the one who had opened his heart to her.

He just did not know how.

But this . . .

As she became accustomed to him, Conrad pressed for more. Deeper he fell, or they fell together, until he didn't know where he ended and Cait began.

Kissing her was not what he'd expected.

It was so much more. The sound she made, deep in her throat, only encouraged him.

She'd learned quickly, and Conrad took advantage of it. Her lips, so much sweeter than he had imagined. Deeper and deeper, until . . .

"My lord?"

Conrad broke away with the same force he had used to pull her to him.

Their eyes met briefly before he opened the flap of the tent.

"Pardon, my lord," his captain said, not daring to look past him. "One of the men wounded his leg this morn."

"How? We've done nothing but ride all day." His

tone was harsher than normal, but he was desperate to speak to Cait.

"He . . . it appears he scratched it on a branch while . . . while relieving himself, my lord."

"A scratch? You come to me because a man's leg is scratched?"

"'Tis festering, Lord Licheford. He can hardly stand."

A foolish complaint, this early on in their campaign, but he could hardly ignore it. "Attend to him until I come."

"Aye, my lord."

Letting the flap drop, Conrad took in the sight before him. Those damned breeches were much too fitted against her legs. And though her hair was pulled back, her surcoat covering all but her calves, he'd never seen a more enticing picture.

"There is a bedroll there." He nodded to the darkened corner of the small tent. Had he known she would be staying here . . . "It appears we have a wounded man. You can return to Licheford with him in the morning."

She opened her mouth, no doubt to argue, but he would not relent. Cait would not be coming with him to London. He would not risk her.

"I will return if I'm able," he said.

"Conrad, wait."

He was almost through the opening when she said it. Despite himself, Conrad complied.

"Please come back."

A retort nearly flew out of his mouth. He'd asked the same of her, many, many times. Begged her to write to him. Begged her to explain why she'd disappeared. But bitter rebukes would serve no purpose now.

"I am so sorry."

Conrad ignored her beseeching tone, which was nearly enough for him to ignore his duties and stay with her. He would not do this right now.

Leaving, Conrad stalked to the other end of camp, where a crowd gathered around the fool who'd been bested by a branch.

Scattering, the men left him alone with the wounded fool, no doubt sensing his dark mood. There was no physician here. But he didn't need one to see the wound had already festered, dangerously so. After inspecting it, he found Ansel and made arrangements for the man to be sent back to Licheford. Two others would return with him to guard Cait.

Later, much later, he sat by the fire watching as each of the men settled down for the night. Only two remained awake, on guard. They would tend to the fire, watch the camp. The area was relatively safe. Though they'd traveled far south of Licheford, their camp was on the property of a dear friend of his father's. An old man who had no children, despite having tried with three separate wives.

Children.

Unbidden, he envisioned Cait sitting in his bed, holding a babe, their babe.

He could go to her now, but Conrad knew it would make it near impossible to keep the vow he'd made to Terric. He'd been alone with her for mere moments earlier, and he'd kissed her in a way no man should kiss a noblewoman, other than her husband.

Please come back.

He was not punishing her for the pain she'd caused him. Staying away was the honorable thing to do.

Though I am not glad for how it happened, nothing pleases me more than your friendship with my brother. He speaks so often of you and the others that it sometimes angers my brother. Rory and Terric may be twin brothers, but they are so very different. But you. More than any of the others, you are most like him. Honorable, decisive. Though Terric will admit he is more even-tempered than you. Someday I would like to see it, these legendary Licheford outbursts. Did your father truly threaten the king with two hundred lanced knights if he harmed your cousin?

He smiled, remembering his response, a missive telling Cait that, aye, indeed, the story was true. And that he never wished her to see his outbursts, though they were, inarguably, milder than his father's. In truth, he'd learned to control them better for that very reason.

Conrad had become a better man. For Cait.

But she'd never known, because she had never come to see him. Until now.

Do not do it. Do not tempt yourself this way.

Conrad had gotten to his feet without realizing he intended to do so, and he could no sooner sit back down than he could watch his country, his people, suffer for the injustices of a cruel and corrupt king. He moved toward the tent even as he told his legs to stop.

He opened the flap and stared down at the slight figure lying atop his bedroll, a blanket tossed over her.

Leave. Now.

But he did not. And when she turned toward him, enough moonlight shone through the opening in the canvas tent for Conrad to see her more clearly than he had in days.

He still loved Cait Kennaugh. Had, in fact, never stopped loving her.

And she was here in his tent. Alone.

God save him, for he would most certainly need saving after this night.

CHAPTER 14

Staring at the side of the tent, Cait touched her fingers to her lips. She'd done so at least a dozen times since Conrad had left. Would he come back? She so badly wanted him to, but it was late, and he was stubborn. While he was gone, she'd snuck out to retrieve her belongings and then removed the tight surcoat Sabine had found for her. The garment had been too tight around her breasts for her to sleep in it. Perhaps she'd wear her riding gown tomorrow, now that she'd revealed herself.

If he lets you stay.

She ran her fingers over lips, remembering how his lips had felt. Never had she imagined kissing Conrad would feel so . . . wicked. Colin had kissed her, twice in fact, but he hadn't used his tongue either time. In fact, it was after that second kiss, in the stables of Bradon Moor, that she'd decided to return to England.

Her brother had been preparing for the voyage for days. The idea, once it had taken root, had refused to leave her thoughts. She'd penned a quick note to her mother and left. That time, she was not the only woman in the group. Cait had gotten farther because of it—she'd blended in with the other wives, although they had, of course, known she was among them.

A blast of air at her back announced his arrival.

Conrad was back.

She sat up, reaching a hand out to him lest he leave before speaking to her. But there seemed little chance of that. He took a few steps toward her and stood over her, watching as if he wished to speak. But he did not.

Cait moved to the edge of the bedroll and patted the space beside her.

Conrad shook his head.

She slid to the other end of the bedroll, where her feet had been, and patted the empty space again.

He paused, for just a moment, and then he sat.

A faint smell of smoke drifted toward her. So he'd sat by the fire after tending to the wounded man. Had he considered not coming back to her?

"I thought perhaps you'd not come."

His look said he nearly had not.

"I would not blame you. It was wretched of me not to write to you. Not to explain."

He didn't make a sound.

This time, Cait had thought of what she would say. In fact, she'd thought of little else since their talk in the buttery, and while she did not have the answers he sought, not precisely, she would try her best to explain.

"I did not . . ." She pulled her legs underneath her. "I knew I did not deserve you."

It was much easier to say these things in her head than it was to share them with Conrad when he sat so near, looking weary, interested, and extremely handsome. He'd always been the most assured man Cait had ever known. Even more so than Terric, if such a thing were possible.

How had she ever had the courage to ask this man to meet her privately?

"You are a man whose legend grew every time my brother spoke of your feats . . . your ideas. When your father died"—how did she explain this?—"you became an earl."

His brows drew together, but otherwise, Conrad said nothing.

"I am the only daughter, the sister, of a chief. After what happened, my brother became even more protective of me. I . . . trusted no one, save my family. Save you. Words have never come easily to me, even when they're required."

"When you wrote, they came easily enough." His harsh tone startled her. How could she know him so well, and not at all?

"One of the reasons, I think, for the letters. I'd never spoken with anyone, even in my family, so openly. Although we hadn't spent much time together in person, I felt as if I could confess anything to you, and you'd write to reassure me."

These weren't the words she'd practiced.

"I mean to say . . ."

"Why did you come now, Cait?"

She licked her lips and noticed his eyes darken with desire. But Cait had not meant it as a provocation. She was simply unsure how to form the words. How to explain herself when her attention was so diverted by the solid, handsome presence at the other end of her bedroll.

Just say it. Say it!

"I do not want to marry Colin MacGregor."

That was not quite *it*.

"So you came to escape an unwanted marriage?" he asked, anger flickering across his expression.

Nay! Ugh, he was maddening.

"I came because . . ."

Say it, Cait. You may never have another chance.

"I came because I never stopped . . ."

Loving you. Loving you. You told him already, in the buttery. Just say it again.

"I did not stop writing because I did not care." *Coward.* "Or because I did not want for you to write back. Those letters were everything, are everything, to me."

Then he did something she didn't expect. Conrad reached for her, pulling her against his chest. His arms wrapped around her, and Cait never, ever wanted him to let go.

"You stopped writing because you cared more for me than you did yourself."

He said it so quietly, Cait had to strain to hear each word.

It was true, of course. She'd hated herself for something that people kept telling her was not her fault. Conrad. Her new friends. They'd all told her she was not to blame, but in her heart she didn't believe it. Even now, sitting with Conrad and admitting this to him, she still didn't believe it.

She looked up, pulling away just enough to see his face.

In answer to the silent questions in her eyes—Did he understand? Did he forgive her?—Conrad leaned down and kissed her.

But this was unlike their first kiss, so soft and gentle it was hard to believe it was the same man. She opened for him as his tongue demanded entry, but even then it coaxed softly, moving in perfect rhythm with his lips as they glided over hers.

The long, slow kiss she wished would never end eventually did, Conrad watching her like she was a peregrine on his wrist, about to fly away.

Forgive me. Forgive me. Love me the way you once did.

He kissed her forehead and held her once more, answering her in his own way. She wasn't sure exactly what this meant, and surely there was more that needed to be discussed, but being in his arms right now reminded Cait of why she'd first fallen in love with him so many years ago.

He was exactly who she wanted to be. Strong. Assured. And there was hope for them yet. She loved him still, had never stopped.

And I think he still loves me too.

CHAPTER 15

"You are a vile, wretched man, Lord Licheford." It was not what Cait had imagined saying to Conrad after she'd slept in his arms all night. But she'd woken up alone, and it had soon become clear that he still intended to send her away.

After dressing, she'd made her way to the fire. Conrad smiled at her, and she could do naught but smile back. But before she even had an opportunity to say, "Good morn," she noticed the three men already mounted, ready to leave. Her horse at the ready.

"No," she had said simply.

"Cait Kennaugh," Conrad said, too quietly. His men pretended to busy themselves with packing up the camp, but she caught their surreptitious glances. They were listening. "You are going back to Licheford with them. 'Tis too dangerous, where we are going."

She opened her mouth to argue when he added, "Besides, 'tis not proper."

That garnered more looks from some of the men. She ignored them.

"I will not go."

There, it was a simple matter. He'd asked. She'd answered.

"You will go with them or find yourself hauled atop your mount."

His calm tone made his remark all the more infuriating, but it was his next remark that elicited her appraisal of him as *vile* and *wretched*.

"And," he added happily, "if you do not, I will tell your brother when we meet about the matter of Timmy . . ."

She gasped. "You would not?"

His grin said otherwise.

Timmy was a brown hare she'd captured after Terric had steadfastly refused to train her. Cait had begged both her brothers, not caring which weapon they chose. The sword. Dagger. Bow. She'd just wanted to learn how to protect herself. While Rory had somewhat relented, Terric had refused. Said the training yard was no place for her and that it was the men's job to protect the women.

And so Cait had found her new pet, Timmy. If her brother had been terrified of rabbits since he was a wee babe, that was not Cait's concern. She made sure everyone knew she was enraptured with the wee thing, and insisted the rabbit accompany her everywhere. Timmy had also found himself accidentally locked inside Terric's bedchamber on more than one occasion.

She'd told him a servant must have done it.

Only she, and Conrad, knew differently.

Perhaps *vile* and *wretched* were a mite too strong, but he was certainly not above using her secrets against her. If Conrad did not play fair, well . . . neither would she.

Turning on her heels, Cait made her way back to

the tent before she could think too long on it. Knowing he would be along any moment, she tossed off her mantle, pretending for just one moment that she were Roysa. That she was bold enough to make the man she loved desire her.

When he pulled back the flap, she waited for him to come close. Then, before she could think on what she was doing, Cait opened her mouth ever so slightly and stared at his lips. It was easy to remember how he'd made her feel last eve, when his mouth had slammed against hers. How his tongue had guided her lips to open.

When she bit her bottom lip, it was unplanned. As was the shiver that ran through her when Conrad stared at her *that way*.

"It will not work."

Cait did not believe him.

She took a step forward.

"We've much to yet"—another step closer—"discuss."

Cait did not relent, even for a moment. She would not retreat to Licheford. Not now.

Not ever.

She'd retreated for entirely too long.

"Mmm. To discuss." He watched her, rightfully leery.

"Aye," she said, hardly listening. Instead, she stared at his chest, wondering what it looked like bare. What it would feel like pressed against her.

Cait was not ignorant of the ways of men and women, having been raised with two brothers. Neither did she know precisely what lovemaking was like. But she intended to learn.

With him.

"I am not going back," she said, with all the authority she imagined an earl's wife would muster. "I am staying with you, just as the other women are staying with their husbands."

One final step closed the distance between them.

"'Tis true, you prepare for a fight. Perhaps the biggest of your life. But I am also preparing, and will not be waylaid."

They were so close now Cait had to lift her chin to continue looking into his eyes.

"What," he asked dryly, "are you preparing for, Cait?"

Last eve, she'd stopped short of saying all of what she'd intended to say. She would not make that same mistake again. This was her chance, finally, to fight for what she wanted. If she allowed it to pass her by, she might find herself back in the prison that was Bradon Moor, thinking of what might have been.

"I am preparing to become your wife."

His eyes widened.

"To learn how to please you. To rediscover the man I once knew, and learn how he's changed. But mostly, I am preparing—I am prepared—to love you. As I have from the start. By giving you all of me, Conrad. As I should have done years ago."

Oddly, the words did not stick in her mouth. Nor did they make her feel exposed. Vulnerable. Although the feelings of unworthiness that had made her pull away from him still assailed her, she realized she had made a grave mistake by punishing herself, and in turn, punishing him.

"Let me love you, Conrad."

At first, she thought he'd deny her. Send her back as crushed as he had likely been when she'd stopped responding to his letters. One moment, she looked up at him, waiting. The next, she was hauled against his chest so quickly Cait lost her breath.

His kiss was hard, maybe even punishing for the

years they'd lost. Ones she had thrown away. But as he claimed her mouth, Cait could not regret that lost time because she was in his arms now.

"I will not go," she whispered between fevered kisses.

He kissed her again.

She allowed it, but she'd let too many words stay unspoken, for too long. The time for silence had ended. "I will not, Conrad. Unless you say you do not want me. If I go, I return to Bradon Moor. Not Licheford."

Cait held her breath. Although she hadn't intended to make such a statement, she was surprised to realize she meant it. If he sent her away now, this was the end of their long journey together.

His jaw flexed, and Cait's heart leapt in his moment of indecision. She didn't regret the words, but every bit of her understood what his answer would mean to them both.

When he spoke, she resisted the urge to grip onto his shirt as if the ground would swallow her otherwise.

CHAPTER 16

He knew what she was asking.

And if Cait had not stopped writing, the answer would be an easy one. Indeed, if he'd had his choice, he would have married Cait long ago. He'd told this woman things he'd told none other, including his Broken Blade brothers.

He should have gone to her, gone to Bradon Moor. Conrad realized that now, but he'd been too stubborn, too proud, to make the journey without knowing why she'd stopped writing.

Let me love you, Conrad.

He wanted nothing more in this world than to do just that. They still had much to discuss, to overcome. But he could see the resolve in her expression.

Cait would not turn back, no matter how loud his protestations, unless he let her go. And he would be damned if he'd do that.

"Your brother will kill me," he said once again, and meant it. Although Terric had brought Roysa with him, he'd done so reluctantly, and Conrad and Cait weren't married.

She smiled, understanding what this meant.

"When I tell you of his courtship with Roysa, you'll feel much reassured."

"You will not come inside the city." On this, he would stand firm. "If we need to take it by force—"

"I understand."

He wasn't sure that she did.

"Cait . . ."

Conrad couldn't find the words. He'd never struggled to do so before. Not with his men, his household, or even with her for those many years they had corresponded. But this version of Cait, so achingly familiar yet not, silenced him as if he were a green boy.

She reached up and cupped his face. The gesture was so simple, so powerful, and it struck Conrad that no one had touched him in such a way—comforting, loving—since his mother had died. His relations with Lady Threston and others like her had been purely sensual in nature.

"I do not want to go back to Bradon Moor. I do not want to marry Colin MacGregor. It took me many years to find the courage to come here, to tell you this. I want you and none other. And I will spend every day of this journey apologizing for the hurt I caused you—and us—by not saying as much sooner. Terric will understand. I will make him understand."

Satisfied, more than satisfied, Conrad placed his hands over hers.

"We are in the midst of a rebellion."

Cait blinked. "I know it well."

Of course she did. Cait had been at Dromsley during the attack. The thought of how close she'd come to danger . . .

"You asked me to let you love me," he said, the words coming more easily now. The love in her eyes, her confidence in him, emboldened him to take a stand. "If I agree, you must allow me to do the same."

It seemed such a simple thing, to allow another person to give you love. But if Cait's hesitation were any indication, she understood the true meaning of his question.

She'd spent so many years hiding, from others, from herself, and berating herself for something that wasn't her fault. For something that couldn't be changed. Could she truly allow him back inside? Conrad had seen the way she interacted with the others. Knew, even back then, how difficult it was for her to share herself.

Conrad could not completely understand her reticence, but he would try to be patient with her. Would rely on the knowledge that she'd opened herself to him before, in the form of a letter.

"I will try," she said finally.

Conrad supposed that was good enough, for now.

* * *

"Welcome to Lennox, my lord."

The countess looked at Cait, likely attempting to ascertain her rank and role. She and Conrad had discussed their plan earlier, knowing they'd be met with this same question at each castle or manor they visited on the way to London.

It was unheard of for an unmarried woman to travel alone with all men. No chaperone. No reason to be present among so many knights and soldiers. Some would call her a camp follower, a prostitute, for that alone.

Conrad bowed like a man who had learned to do so in the cradle.

"My lady," he replied. They stood before her in the

great hall of Lennox Castle, rather small but well-appointed. It was important, Conrad had said, for them to secure the countess's support. Her husband, who had signed the order's letter to the king, had since died. Lady Lennox would decide whether or not to send her men to march with Conrad, a show of support that may tip the scales, for the late Lord Lennox had been one of King John's longtime supporters . . . until he'd felt compelled to take a stand against him.

"Allow me to introduce Lady Cait Kennaugh, sister of the chief of Clan Kennaugh in the borderlands, and Earl of Dromsley. She is my intended."

Cait did not show the wily Lady Lennox her surprise, but her chest clenched at Conrad's words. Intended?

That had not been their plan.

"I fear her chaperone was injured last eve, necessitating the woman's return to Licheford."

That much, while not entirely true, had been rehearsed. But they'd decided she would be introduced as his cousin, not his intended. What was he about? Injured or nay, a woman not related to Conrad, traveling with him . . .

And of course Lady Lennox looked at her with suspicion.

Ignoring Conrad's marshal, who cleared his throat behind them, no doubt uncomfortable with the lie, Cait met and held the gaze of the elderly Lady Lennox, after bowing, of course.

Conrad was right, after all, she was the only sister of a man who was both a chieftain and an earl. And she had done nothing improper, yet. She'd not be set down by anyone, including this recently widowed countess.

"I am very sorry to hear of your chaperone's injury," the countess said. "Was it a serious one?"

"Not so that she will be unable to recover quickly, I do hope. She scratched her leg on a branch."

"It festered," Ansel blurted behind her.

Aware he should not have spoken yet, the marshal immediately apologized. And Cait tried not to smile at the man's clumsy attempt at support. She would be sure to thank him later.

"You and your chaperone are brave indeed, to join Lord Licheford and his men on such a dangerous mission."

Though the countess spoke to her, Conrad answered. "My lady is very much so, but I fear her chaperone's constitution was not as hearty as hers."

Cait tried desperately not to smile. The poor man Conrad spoke of had endured many jests this morn about his run-in with a branch. Poor man. He'd only recently been knighted.

Lady Lennox did not comment. She did, however, finally allow them to leave.

"I've had rooms prepared. And we shall speak after supper, Lord Licheford. If that is agreeable to you?"

"It is." Conrad bowed again. "You do us a great honor, my lady."

Cait did not like her.

She may be wealthy. And powerful. And a woman. Cait liked nothing better than to see another woman in a position of power. And yet, she could tell this woman judged her.

Attempting to ignore her feelings, for the sake of their cause, Cait smiled broadly.

"Many thanks, Lady Lennox, for your hospitality."

The countess did not return her smile. Her only response was a murmur that Cait could not even hear.

Following a chambermaid from the hall, Cait kept

her expression neutral until she was shown to a small room—directly beside Conrad's. The girl gestured for her to step inside, and with nothing to recommend her staying in the passageway, she did so. But not before she caught Conrad's eye, the promise there making her shiver.

They'd ridden beside each other all day, only stopping once. They'd talked, laughed, and likely bewildered the men with their most unusual situation. But there was tension between them too—different than it had been before. The look he gave her now promised the kisses they'd shared were just the beginning of all that he could teach her.

Would he come to her tonight?

Did she want him to after what he had just done?

Conrad's intended.

Instead of meeting his sly grin with one of her own, Cait gave him a look that told him he would answer for what he'd said. And the cad simply widened his smile, accepting the challenge and issuing one of his own.

CHAPTER 17

"**M**y lord?"

Conrad lifted his head from his hands as Ansel entered his bedchamber. He watched his longtime advisor sink into the chair beside him, the fine leather creaking under his weight. Light from both the fire and numerous candles illuminated an opulent but small room.

He'd sent for the marshal immediately after the long, torturous evening meal, which he'd spent navigating the countess, followed by a private meeting with her in the solar.

In truth, he wanted nothing more than to be alone with Cait so he could explain his decision for altering their planned story. So he could speak with her more about her reasons for never telling Terric about their correspondence, for deciding to stop writing. He wanted to move past it, but he found he could not. Not yet.

But most of all he wanted to touch her. Feel her in his arms. Love her for as long as possible before her brother cut his short life in London. For Conrad had no doubt his friend would kill him if he dishonored his sister. He'd not do so intentionally, of course. But the prospect of waiting until they were wed before making her his . . .

Conrad had learned restraint at an early age, but their forced proximity on this journey did not bode well. She waited in the chamber next to them, and only one matter could keep Conrad from her.

"I spoke with the countess after the evening meal. She will not provide men."

Ansel's mouth dropped open. "Her husband . . . he was one of your first supporters."

Indeed. And he'd assumed she would have another pressing reason for supporting their cause. Although Lady Lennox's husband had initially served King John, her father had served another royal: King Philip II of France. Indeed, the two families were so close, Philip's son, the future king of France, was considered a family friend. It would be to their advantage to blunt John's powers, and ultimately his ability to continue the war no one wanted.

On behalf of his wife, the late earl had already made contact with Philip, who was well aware of the events unfolding in England. Lady Lennox was to be their door to the French king—a fail-safe they could rely upon should their stand in London be in vain. If she refused to help them, others would do the same.

"I know it well."

Ansel looked as bereft as Conrad felt. "What reason did she give?"

Conrad made a sound of disgust. "She fears King John's wrath if our campaign should fail."

"So she would prefer to allow the king to drain her coffers in taxes to fund a war against her friends in France?"

"Apparently so."

They sat, and drank, in silence.

Since he'd left the countess, Conrad had spent

every single moment strategizing, thinking of someone powerful enough to fill the void she had created. He could think of only one person who possessed as much influence as Lady Lennox, who could speak to the French king on their behalf. If they secured his support, they would be facing King John on an even battleground.

Thus far, they'd not spoken to him. Had not asked for his support.

With good reason. He had been Conrad's father's greatest enemy.

"Stanton, Kenshire, Clave, Noreham, FitzWalter. . . ," he said slowly, contemplatively, "for every signature we've obtained, for all those marching south with us, none will matter if our tenuous ties to France are not reinforced."

Ansel looked up to the ceiling, as if knowing he'd not approve of Conrad's next words.

"We've no choice."

His marshal still did not understand.

"If we think to force the king's hand by taking London peaceably, without the support of Lady Lennox, we need him."

"No."

Conrad would have smiled at Ansel's adamant tone were his marshal's concern not valid.

"Aye."

He waited for Ansel to see they had no other alternative.

"You will take the men south, to Heath Castle, and bring word to the others of my delay."

"My lord, 'tis madness. He is as like to murder you as to offer the support you seek. Your father will rise from his grave to kill you himself."

It was a true enough statement. If his father had been alive, he would indeed have forbidden the action Conrad was about to take. And it wouldn't matter if Conrad reminded him of the petty nature of the fight that lasted for decades. Or if he explained that Lord Lindemere's support was necessary for the success of their rebellion. And to ensure he and the others did not face the king's wrath for having defied him.

But Conrad agreed with Ansel about one thing.

None of that would have mattered to his father. He would have preferred to lose the war than treat with the man who had been responsible for his nephew's near brush with death. It was Lord Lindemere's complaint, and his cousin's subsequent tangle with the king, that had caused him to bring two hundred lanced men to court. That had nearly resulted in his father being expelled.

But Conrad was not his father.

"Choose no more than four men to accompany me. Tell Terric and the others we should not be delayed by more than a sennight."

Ansel glared at him in response.

"We have no choice." Conrad stood.

"And Lady Cait?"

Would she still be awake? Likely not at this hour, but he would soon find out.

"She comes with me."

CHAPTER 18

Two men rode in front of them, two behind them. The sun had not yet made an appearance, but despite the chill, Cait shrugged off her mantle. She wanted to feel the air touch her skin. Despite the brevity of their stay at Lennox Castle, it felt like they'd been cooped up inside for too long.

She'd woken early after a fitful sleep, disappointed that Conrad had not visited her last eve as he'd promised, only to break her fast in the great hall under the sting of the countess's intense scrutiny. Cait could not have left the hall quickly enough.

As they passed the gatehouse, Cait looked around for the other men, assuming their retinue would be joining them. But there were no mounted knights and supply carts. Indeed, no one followed them at all.

"The others?"

She peered ahead, sitting higher in her saddle, but still, nothing.

"Left at dawn. To London."

Cait didn't hide her confusion. "Why are we not traveling with them?"

Conrad seemed different this morn. Something was not quite well.

"I met with the countess privately last eve after the meal. She has pulled her support."

Oh dear.

"Without it, I fear Londoners may not welcome us as we'd hoped."

"France," Cait muttered. She understood how important it was for the order to have a connection to the French king's heir apparent. Even the appearance of one might be enough for them to successfully capture London and force King John's hand.

"As such, the others will continue on to London. We're headed to Lindemere Castle."

Cait gasped. Surely she had misheard.

"Lindemere?"

"We've no other choice. The countess assured me her ties to France will still serve us if necessary, but without a public show of support, that fact hardly matters."

"So Lindemere . . ."

Cait thought back to that particular missive. The one where Conrad had shared the saga of his cousin. Lord Lindemere had coveted the man's bedchamber at court, and so he'd had his belongings removed, without permission, and taken the more prominent room for himself. The situation had escalated, and Conrad's cousin had been arrested, and nearly beheaded, for his part in the matter. Which had led to his father's famous gambit of bringing two hundred armed men to court.

After the incident, the former earl's relationship with the king had obviously been strained. It had become even more so after he refused the earl and countess's request to cure them of the illness known as the king's evil, which some said could be healed with a touch from the king. Although she doubted the veracity of such claims, the insult could not be denied.

"Aye. Lindemere. I came to you last eve to mention it, but you were asleep."

That pulled Cait from her reverie.

"You came?" She didn't try to hide her surprise. Or her pleasure.

"You were asleep, I assume. I met with Ansel well into the night."

Cait had been so consumed with thoughts of them, of her and Conrad, she'd forgotten temporarily they were in the midst of a rebellion. Although she'd waited for him to come, fretted over it, she had never imagined such complications could be the cause for his delay.

"I did not realize," she mumbled.

"You assumed I had not come?"

Glancing from his profile to the dusty Roman road on which they traveled, Cait admitted as much. "'Twould be no less than I deserved."

His silence, she assumed, was Conrad's way of agreeing with her.

But as a pair of riders approached them, Conrad transformed before her eyes—one moment, he was simply a man, albeit a dangerously handsome one, the next a knight. He greeted the two men stiffly, positioning himself in front of Cait. Neither man appeared particularly ominous, but the fierce look on Conrad's face startled her.

As soon as the men were out of earshot, he shouted to the riders in front of them.

"Ride ahead and see if there are others."

"Others?" Cait asked, puzzled. From what she'd seen, there was every indication the men were alone.

Conrad waited for the men to comply before turning to her.

"Thieves. I would be assured they are alone and do not plan to surround us."

She and her brother had passed more than one group of border reivers on the journey from Bradon Moor, but they had been easily identifiable with their hobblers and padded gambesons. The men who'd passed them had looked nothing like that.

"How do you know they are thieves?" she asked, genuinely curious.

"Just an inclination."

"Riders!" came the shout from ahead of them. Then all at once, chaos broke out.

"Over there," Conrad yelled to her, his expression fierce. She complied immediately, spurring her mare off the road and closer to the tree line.

Instead of moving forward, as she'd expected, Conrad fell back. She could hear the scraping of his sword against its sheath and then shouts.

Cait tried not to think back. To remember. But she could not help but do so.

Moments later, Conrad reappeared with the two Licheford men who had ridden behind them. They ignored her, flying ahead and around the bend in front of them.

More shouts ripped through the air. But there were no sounds of battle.

And then silence fell.

With her mount dancing under her, Cait waited for what seemed like an eternity. Finally, Conrad and all four of his men returned, all of them looking very nonplussed.

"'Twill be a long walk," one of the men commented, Conrad muttering a curse under his breath.

"A long walk?" Cait realized, then found that her hands were shaking.

Moments later, Conrad rode up to her, grabbing

the bridle of her horse and guiding her mount forward.

"She's untrained for battle," he said by way of explanation, nodding to her mare.

And then, as if nothing had happened, the others resumed their previous positions and their party rode ahead, Conrad speaking softly to her horse and then finally letting go as they trotted along.

"As are you," he said, and it took a moment for her to understand. "Training. Experience. They teach us how to recognize thieves who are very likely attempting to surround and rob us."

To surround and rob us.

"They'll not attack anyone else this day," he continued.

Her heart stuck in her throat. "Do you mean . . ."

But even as she spoke, Cait spotted them. Four men walking on the road ahead of them. No horses. And from what she could tell as they approached, no weapons either. Cait glanced at Conrad for clarification, and that was when she noticed it. A second sword hanging on his left side. Each of the Licheford knights had an extra one.

She could not help but look at the thieves on foot as they passed them on horseback, even though Conrad and his men did not pay them any mind. The murderous glares they gave her back forced a shudder from her.

"They do not appear very pleased," she said finally to Conrad.

"They still live," was all he said.

Cait looked back, wondering how long they'd continue to do so. With no inn nor village nearby, those men would just as likely starve as they would live to steal another day. But she remained silent as the woods become less dense, giving way to open moorland as far as she could see.

It was only later, after her breathing had returned to normal, that she chanced another glance at Conrad. Her eyes landed on his scar.

"I am sorry for it," she said, realizing the man who'd reacted so quickly back there was hardly the one she'd first met all those years ago. Not yet knighted, slightly more than a boy.

He'd lost what remained of his innocence that day, but then again, so had she.

He seemed to know exactly what she spoke of.

"I know it. And I would do it again, every day of my life, if 'twas necessary."

He looked at her. Not past her, but at her.

"I've never been ashamed of it," he said, speaking of his scar. "It may have scared away some women—"

"Good," she blurted without thinking.

Conrad smiled. "And mayhap a would-be attacker too. But not once have I thought of it as anything less than part of me. Part of the man I quickly became after that day."

They'd never spoken of it directly before, and hearing him say those words, and seemingly mean them, made Cait feel slightly better for having been the source of his disfigurement.

"It does make you look quite fierce. Especially when you scowl so."

His scowl deepened. "I do no such thing."

If only he could see himself.

"You do. Whenever you are displeased."

"As I should be now. We ride to the manor of a man with little honor to beg for a favor he'll be disinclined to grant us. My friends travel to London to attempt something that has never been done before, a peaceful coup against our king. We were set upon by thieves. And most importantly, I was robbed of an evening alone with a woman who stubbornly refuses to take herself back to safety."

"However?" She could sense there was more to this story.

"However . . ." All traces of Conrad's scowl disappeared, his gaze intense and . . . something more. Cait's insides clenched in anticipation of his next words. "There's much to look favorably upon as well."

Her heart skipped a beat. "Such as?"

"Such as"—Conrad moved his mount closer toward hers—"such as tonight. When we can have that discussion, finally."

Again, she clenched tightly at the words he did not say.

"Discussion . . . ?"

"Aye, my lady. The one where I show you precisely what you've missed these past years hiding away at Bradon Moor."

Cait's breath caught at his implication.

That kiss had been such a small taste, one that had merely left her ravenous for more.

"I . . . I've missed you," she said sincerely.

"Oh no, Lady Cait. You've little notion of what you have missed when you stopped corresponding with me." But his tone wasn't bitter, as it had been just a few days earlier, and he ended with a grin. "But I plan to rectify that. This eve."

CHAPTER 19

Cait sat across from him, the only space available, atop a log that appeared to have been strategically placed there for her. They'd made camp, and Cait had ducked into Conrad's tent to change into the hose and loose linen shirt Sabine had found. By the time she returned, the men had already taken seats around the fire.

Although the day had been cool, the night remained somehow temperate. A full moon, coupled with a cloudless sky, offered as beautiful a night as Cait had seen since leaving Bradon Moor.

"I hadn't realized the sky could be so beautiful here."

The men looked at her.

"In England," she said hesitantly. Not wanting them to think she disparaged their home, Cait clarified, "'Tis lovely here. I . . ." She stopped, Conrad's grin contagious.

"Our village healer," said Jeffrey, a man sitting next to her, "said that if a male child is born on the fifth day after a new moon, he will be virtuous and loyal, courageous and steadfast. He will be physically healthy and live long."

Conrad rolled his eyes. "Were you born on the fifth day after the new moon, Jeffrey?"

Cait tried not to laugh. The young man seemed very sincere in his belief.

"I was." He lifted his chin, and his flagon.

"I wonder . . ." She accepted a bit of roasted chicken, wondering where they'd gotten the meat. The crated chickens that had come with them from Licheford had been sent along to London with the men, and they had no permits to hunt on this land. "What would your healer have said if the babe was a female?"

Jeffery looked decidedly guilty and offered no response. He was prompted by a kick from the man seated next to him. Was his name Godwin?

"Uh. Well. If it is a female, she will be virile, quarrelsome, and vindictive, but honest nevertheless."

Conrad burst out laughing, and Cait somehow kept a straight face.

"Quarrelsome and vindictive?"

"Aye, my lady," Jeffery rushed to explain, "but I do not believe it to be so."

"But honest," Conrad managed across from her. His eyes danced in the moonlight, and Cait wished more than anything that she were closer to him.

"And virile," Godwin added. "A man would be so lucky to have such a woman."

Their laughter rang out, but it was decidedly at Jeffrey's expense, and Cait took pity on the poor lad.

"I jest with you," she said. "I do believe the moon has many special powers." Cait shifted on the log under her. "But this is certainly not one."

"Besides"—Conrad stretched his legs out in front of him and looked at Jeffrey—"I need no moon to tell me you are both virtuous and loyal."

It was stated casually, but Cait could tell Jeffrey

did not take it so. The young man beamed as if his lord had just offered high praise, which indeed he had.

For the rest of the meal, she listened to the men's banter and sometimes participated in it, but her eyes continued to stray to Conrad. In the few days since she'd come to Licheford, Cait had seen plenty of evidence to suggest he was a man of grace and honor, that he still possessed the very qualities she'd fallen for all those years ago.

And she had nearly let him go.

When their eyes met, Conrad's words, once again, came back to her.

But I plan to rectify that. This eve.

She could tell he must be thinking the same, but neither of them moved. Instead, he continued to converse with his men, all the while watching her. By the time Conrad stood, Cait wasn't sure if her legs would carry her.

Holding out his hand, Conrad stood before her. She could feel the others' eyes on them, but Cait had dispensed with any notions of propriety when she and the women had concocted their plan. She took his hand and rose, expecting him to release her once she did. Instead, Conrad wove his fingers through hers. If he'd not already announced their relationship to the countess the day before, such a display would have surely done so to the men who were watching them.

He led her to the tent and lifted the flap, only then releasing her so she could enter. It struck her then that they hadn't spoken of his words to Lady Lennox, which surely hadn't helped shore up his relations with the woman. It would be best if they stuck to the cousin façade in the future.

"We should speak of what you said to Lady—"

He spun her around. Two hands grasped the sides of her face as Conrad's lips silenced the remainder of her words. He kissed her so deeply, and so thoroughly, that she completely forgot about everything, save the feel of him.

When his hands dropped to her waist, Cait held them there. She wanted to be even closer, to feel the warmth of his skin. When he reached up to cup her breasts, she moaned under his touch, keeping her own hands over his.

Conrad broke off then, looking down at his own hands. When he closed his eyes and moaned, she thought at first it was a sound of pleasure, until he looked at her again. Dropping his hands, he looked at her as if it were the first time he'd seen her that eve.

"What is it?"

When he stepped away, Cait could hardly see him, though she could hear him moving in the dark.

"Conrad?"

No answer. She could see him lower to the ground, to the bedroll she'd laid out earlier.

"Come here," he said, his voice husky.

She sat next to him, Conrad's face illuminated just barely from the moonlight seeping in through the tent's walls.

"Lie with me."

Confused, Cait pulled off her boots and tossed them aside. She turned to him then, her gaze drawn to the opening in his linen shirt.

"Do not look at me so," he said, reaching up to tuck her hair behind her ear.

But Cait could not hide the desire he'd awoken in her. Indeed, she didn't wish to try.

"Perhaps this will be better."

Pulling her down next to him, her back to him,

Conrad positioned her so that her head was tucked just below his, against his chest.

"I'd have easily taken you, here in a tent, unwed." One arm wrapped around her shoulders. "I do not think when you're near. It has always been so. From that very first day."

The honor she'd always admired in him nearly choked her now, knowing it was responsible for the dousing of the fire he had ignited.

How had she not guessed that straightaway?

"I'd easily have *been* taken. Here. In a tent. Unwed," she admitted.

Cait clasped her hand over his.

"'Tis not what you deserve."

Cait had many thoughts about what she deserved, but none of them were worth mentioning now. She knew he would not wish to hear them.

"Because I am Terric's sister."

His silence was her answer.

"Even if we are betrothed?"

"But we are not . . ."

She could feel his breath on her neck.

"I am sorry for lying to the countess."

"Are you?"

More silence. Then, "No, I am not. The way she looked at you . . . she acted as if your presence was improper."

"'Tis more than improper, as well you know."

"That matters not. She could have hidden her derision. And so I spoke without thinking, daring her to voice her objections."

Every bit of anger she'd felt slipped away.

"Do you believe"—Cait hated to even think of it —"that her decision to withdraw public support may have been prompted by it?"

If her decision to come had harmed their cause . . .

"Nay, I do not."

Though his firm tone alleviated her concern a bit, a small bit of doubt remained.

Conrad had pulled a blanket over them, but Cait's hands and nose still felt cold. She backed into him a bit more, telling herself it was merely because she was cold. The scent of sandalwood and hint of campfire surrounded her, oddly comforting.

"I did not intend to cause any harm with my presence," she began. "I simply . . ."

"You simply what, Cait? What did you hope to gain from this?"

That answer, at least, came easily.

"You."

When he exhaled, Cait closed her eyes. "I never should have stopped writing. I should have welcomed you to Bradon Moor long ago. Or come back to a tournament, back to England."

His arms tightened around her. "I understand why you did not. I do not like, or agree, with your reasoning. But I can understand it. And you are here now."

I wasn't too late. Thank you, God, for giving me another chance.

"You knew a man who thought he had rescued you. Who thought he understood his place as the only heir to a great earl, a son to parents more noble than their titles. You knew a man who believed the world was good despite bad people like the one who attacked you."

The man Conrad had killed.

"I *know* that man." Cait turned her head, needing to see him. "That man is you."

As she said the words, she realized they were only partially true. Hadn't she noticed that he'd changed? True, he had the same sauntering gait, the same intense, scrutinizing stare, but the boy she'd known had grown into a man, a man who had been through heartache and sorrow. He'd been betrayed by a woman he'd thought he loved. Had lost both parents and seen his country suffer for the sins of the very person who was supposed to lead them.

"And yet you've grown," she added. "We both have."

"I may perish in the effort," he said, kissing her lips so softly Cait did not even have time to close her eyes before he finished. "But we will begin anew."

Neck straining, Cait laid her head back down, fitting against him as if she had been sleeping there for her entire life.

"We will learn about each other as best we can in the midst of such chaos. And when it is over . . . if you still wish it . . ." Conrad swept her hair away from her neck, kissing the sensitive flesh there. "We will wed."

She wished for nothing more than that very thing.

"Until that time," he continued before she could answer, "though I intended otherwise this eve, and very much wish it could be otherwise"—another kiss, this time closer to her ear—"I will ensure when we reunite with Terric I can say honestly that I've not behaved improperly toward his sister."

Kissing her there did not bode well for his promise. But Cait remained silent. She knew Conrad well enough to understand the futility of mounting any kind of argument. He might be more accommodating than most, but he was still an earl, a man accustomed to getting his way.

And Cait had endured—and won—many battles of will with powerful men. Men who were accustomed to having their authority met with deference.

Her father.

Terric.

And sometimes even Rory.

Arguing with his assessment would yield nothing. He wanted them to learn about each other again, as if they had just met?

Very well.

She had stopped writing. Cait had nearly destroyed any chance of them being together. So she would acquiesce. For now. Or appear to, at least.

"A lovely plan," she murmured, wiggling against him, knowing precisely what the hardness she found there meant. "Then I will say good night, my lord."

Conrad groaned but held her closer still.

Cait smiled into the night, thinking on his words. Conrad may be able to tell Terric truthfully he had not behaved improperly toward her, but *she* had never made such a vow.

And she would most certainly not behave properly toward him.

CHAPTER 20

Cait thought to torture him.

First, she'd opened herself to him in her letters, telling him stories she claimed she'd never shared with anyone else. Like the time she'd hidden both of her brothers' swords from them after unsuccessful attempts to get them to train her. Or not so pleasant memories, like the nightmares she'd endured after the tournament.

He'd felt helpless, so far away from her. But as close to her, in other ways, as he ever had to another person.

When she'd stopped writing, Conrad had nearly gone mad. Her brother had attended the tournament that year, just like always, and he'd nearly told Terric everything, even though it would mean breaking his word to Cait. A comment from Terric had silenced him: he'd claimed his sister finally seemed to "be the same woman she'd been before the attack." Conrad had thought perhaps her correspondence with him had been a reminder of painful memories. It was the only reason he had not gone to Scotland. Why he'd held back.

If she were healing, without him, he would not be

the cause of her pain. Certainly not at the expense of her happiness.

Even so, he'd decided he would not marry anyone else. His parents had died, but not even his mother's memory could force him to fulfill his duty. To marry and extend Licheford's boundaries. His only relationships were with women such as Lady Threston, although his attention was fixed on managing Licheford, and later, the rebellion.

In some ways, he was content.

Was.

But no longer.

She'd come back into his life with all the force of an explosion, her sole purpose to drive him mad, apparently. The way she was looking at him now, as if he were a particularly fine morsel on her plate . . .

After three days . . . three very long days and even longer nights of torture, Conrad did not doubt Cait did it apurpose. At first, he'd not been sure.

The sidelong glance.

A lingering touch.

The way she moved her backside against him as they lay in each other's arms at night. Her attentions were hesitant at first, but she'd gotten bolder. Aside from the evening they'd spent in the inn, in separate bedchambers thankfully, Conrad had hardly slept, courtesy of his very innocent, yet not so innocent, companion.

The men asked no questions, but they knew, of course.

Lady Cait was attempting to kill him before they reached London.

"Stop," he said under his breath, reaching for Cait's hand to help her dismount in front of Lindemere Castle.

She raised her eyebrows as she took his hand,

pretending not to understand. "Apologies, my lord. Have I offended you in some way?"

My lord.

Did Cait even realize that she only used his title when she'd done something impertinent or saucy?

"Nay," he said tightly, ignoring the stares of Lindemere's men as he helped her down and led her toward the keep. It looked as if rain were imminent, so he hurried her inside, following the steward.

The decision to arrive after the meal had been strategic. The less time Lindemere could spend with Cait, the better off they were for it. Although Conrad had never met his father's greatest enemy, he'd heard of him many, many times throughout the years.

Nothing could prepare him for the man he saw as the steward led them into the hall.

The large man with ruddy cheeks and bright white hair wore five, nay six, different colors on his person, one as bright as the next. Could this be the villain who had started a war with his cousin? He looked more like an aging jester than a powerful baron.

Conrad deliberately did not look at Cait, for if he did, surely his training would fail him. If the baron had thought to unbalance Conrad by his manner, he had unfortunately succeeded.

"Lord Licheford, however are you, my son?" the man asked with a big smile as he approached, his tone almost . . . warm.

My son? "I am well, my lord," he said, doing his best to sound both calm and neutral. "If you will allow me to present Lady Cait, sister of Terric Kennaugh, chief of Clan Kennaugh and Earl of Dromsley."

Lindemere waited for Cait to finish her bow.

"Does her brother know?"

Conrad and Cait exchanged a glance.

"Pardon, my lord?" Cait startled.

"That his sister is in love with the very man who thinks to bring an errant king to heel? One who has come, I assume, to ask for support in such a cause."

Conrad was rarely rendered speechless, but he needn't have worried that this was one of the few occasions. The baron quickly filled the void with more words.

"The circumstances that bring an unwed maid and an earl into my hall are curious indeed. But that matters naught, I suppose. You will forgive my mutterings. But her brother is a dear friend of yours, is he not? One of the founding members of your knightly order? The Order of the Broken Blade? I also wonder whose blade it is named for, but that, I fear, is a discussion for another day. Just now your friends are already beginning to arrive in London. You've little time to waste here, in my hall, listening to the ramblings of an old man."

Conrad regained some, though not all, of his composure.

"Lord Lindemere." How had the man learned so much? And why was he not threatening to toss him out of his hall? "We have indeed come to seek your assistance."

Before he finished, the baron waved his hand in the air for Conrad to stop.

"And I will consider giving it, but only if you and Lady Cait join me for a drink."

The former earl's enemy had surprised him in nearly every way possible, but he had no choice but to comply, and so he nodded. In response to an order from the baron, the servants scurried to bring seats to the platform, which was no longer arranged for a meal.

Conrad watched as his men were led from the hall by the steward. Ansel did not appear pleased, but Conrad shook his head in response to his marshal's silent question. Lindemere may be a touch mad, but he was no murderer.

"Sit, dear boy."

The corner of Cait's mouth lifted, and Conrad fought a smile of his own. He could not recall being called "dear boy" even when he was, in fact, a boy.

"Wine or ale?"

They sat on either side of Lindemere, in high-backed chairs as intricately carved as the baron's. Each had taken two servants to carry, and Conrad could understand why as his fingers rested on the arm of his own seat.

"Ale," he said at the same time that Cait asked for wine.

Her favorite drink, he remembered, was hypocras, the spiced wine not as common here as it was north of the border. When the wine goblet was handed to her, Conrad found himself watching as Cait took the first sip. Listening as she murmured an obligatory compliment. He tried not to envision her backside pressed against him in sleep. Or the curve of her waist, the only part of her body he'd dared touch these past days.

How had Lindemere surmised the truth of his connection to Cait so quickly?

The way you look at her, you fool.

Conrad took a sip of the ale he'd been given and turned to Lindemere.

"You are not at all what I expected," he said.

Honesty. Conrad's secret weapon.

Lindemere drank, a dribble of ale getting caught in his white beard. "Hmmm."

"My father had few kind words for you, my lord."

Cait gasped.

Lindemere raised his mug. "Rest in peace."

All three of them drank to his father, despite what Conrad had said.

"If he sat here with us, I'd have few kind words for him. Your father was both rash and temperamental, though only marginally more so than his nephew."

Conrad's cousin Marcus had died years before his parents, and he hardly remembered the man. But he had, of course, heard rumors.

"'Tis true I had his belongings removed from his bedchamber."

Lindemere drank again, prompting both he and Cait to do the same.

"But not to place myself in a position of more prominence, as he claimed."

"I did not come here to discuss a matter so long ago resolved," Conrad began, not wishing to open old wounds.

"Ha! Resolved? You glare at me as if I were some mad old man responsible for his father marching to court with a retinue of lanced knights and nearly getting himself tossed into prison for it."

Conrad's eyes narrowed. "Precisely that."

He glanced at Cait then. Though she stayed silent, he could feel her anger for him. For his family. She knew what the deterioration of his father's kinship with the king had ultimately cost his parents.

"I assure you, my boy, I am not to blame for such an act. Your cousin defiled my daughter and should have been grateful I did not kill him."

Conrad's head snapped back from Cait to the baron.

"What did you say?"

"Defiled. Though she'd granted him permission." Lindemere shrugged. "He was ten years her senior and knew well enough not to do so."

Conrad shook his head. "Father would have made mention of it. He'd never have defended such an act."

"Perhaps. If he had known."

Cait leaned forward. "The earl never knew the reason for your original argument with his nephew?"

Impossible.

And yet the baron shrugged. "My daughter wished for it to be so."

It was true. He said it with such straightforward simplicity. The mad baron, perhaps not so mad as he seemed, looked him directly in the eyes.

"You know well, my dear boy, some things are worth more than your own life. When Sir Marcus flew into a fit of rage that so angered the king, enough to have the man nearly beheaded, your father refused to listen to reason. If he'd not stormed from court, returning with those men, it would have been nothing more than a dispute between two wronged parties, provided, of course, your cousin simply apologized to the king. 'Twas all he required for having disrupted the court. He'd never actually behead a man for such a disruption, despite his threat. Instead . . ." Lindemere shrugged. "It was just as well. The father was no more noble than the son is now."

It took Conrad a moment to realize he spoke of the king.

"You do not care for him?"

Ignoring the rest of what the baron had said, which would take him time to process, he focused on the reason they had come here.

"For the king?" The tone of his question effectively answered Conrad's question.

"Why haven't you joined the rebellion?"

Lindemere rolled his eyes. "I am too old to involve myself in such matters. My daughter's husband will inherit this." He waved his arms to indicate the great hall. "Imagine that. A Frenchman. At Lindemere." He made a sound. "'Tis no better than a Scotsman . . ." He stopped then, peering at Cait. "Begging your pardon, my lady."

From the flash of heat in Cait's eyes, she did not seem inclined to give it. Even so, she nodded as demurely as if he'd not just insulted her.

Conrad withheld comment, waiting for the man's next words.

"Lindemere is lost," the baron continued. "What do I care if England is lost with it?"

He needed to think. To strategize. This was not at all how he'd envisioned this conversation, and frankly, Conrad was at a loss for words.

"Your connection to the French court is well-known," Cait said. "Your support could mean the difference between taking London peaceably, by force, or not at all. If we are forced to call upon the French—"

We. Cait had said we.

Lindemere crossed himself. "All will have been lost."

"But surely it would bring prominence and attention to Lindemere if you were at the center of such an effort," she said.

He raised his mug, considering, and Conrad and Cait exchanged a glance.

"What do I care either way?" the old man finally said. "Let's drink! A toast to your happy union."

If he had been confused before, Conrad was even more so now. He could not decide if this were the wiliest, or craziest, man he'd ever met.

"Our union, my lord?"

"Aye," he said as firmly as a man his age could manage. "You and the lovely Scotswoman. For the insult I've given her, I shall rectify it with the support you seek. Now drink."

He did so gladly.

CHAPTER 21

He knew it was Cait before the door fully opened.

Perhaps he was attuned to her movements after spending the last several days imagining what it would feel like to touch her.

To taste her.

To make Cait his, finally.

He'd effectively avoided a confrontation with her earlier. A chambermaid had escorted her from the hall just before Conrad left to speak with the men. Unfortunately, the same maid had returned, telling him "his lady" was in the chamber adjoining his.

A fact he could have happily gone without knowing.

"Conrad?" she asked, her feet softly padding on the floor.

He groaned, cowardly pulling the coverlet over his head.

"Do you think to avoid me?"

She pulled the cream coverlet down.

"Why would you think such a thing?"

Hands on her hips, the small but fierce Cait Kennaugh glared at him. The lone candle beside his canopied bed shone just enough light for him to see her face.

And her shift.

Though the arms billowed and the shapeless garment hung to the ground, Conrad knew well what was underneath. He'd felt it these past sleepless nights.

He forced his thoughts to the promise he'd made Terric.

Relenting a bit, he sighed. "If you've come to talk so that we might learn more of each other"—he rolled to the side, propping his head on one hand —"you'll find me willing."

"Learn more . . ." He did not like the way she smiled.

No indeed. He did not like it at all.

"Aye, 'tis *precisely* what I've come for, my lord."

"Cait, please."

She took a step toward him.

"It seems I've quickly become accustomed to sleeping by your side." She frowned prettily. "And since there is still so much to learn . . ."

"No," he said, his answer immediate.

"Just for a moment. So that we may speak."

"No."

Crossing her arms, Cait tried again. "You said you've forgiven me."

"And I have. Mostly."

"And that you loved me once."

On that, he would disagree.

"I never stopped loving you," he said seriously, watching her eyes as he said it. Conrad had known the truth of his feelings from the very moment he saw her in his courtyard. She thought he had saved her that day, but really, it was the opposite. His life had been all training. And duty. Lessons for the future earl. His only real friends, scattered throughout the country, only to be seen once a year at the Tournament of the North.

Until a missive from Cait arrived. And with it, hope for a future that was more than acquired estates and praying for a good harvest. A future filled with the same abiding love his parents had felt for each other. A smile in the darkness that his country had descended into.

If he'd taken up its cause so fully, it was because he'd needed something to replace the hole Cait had left.

Aye, he'd loved her always. But that did not mean he could be persuaded to dishonor her now.

When she leaned into the bed, Conrad thought to pull away. But she was too quick. Grabbing his shoulder, she didn't hesitate. Cait kissed him. Her lips were on his before he could form another thought.

He'd taught her well.

Her mouth glided over his, her tongue insistent, sweeping inside with the expertise she'd only just acquired.

And the minx thought to use her knowledge to overcome the barrier he'd placed between them. Except Conrad had been seduced before, by women who hoped to claim their place as his countess, and he'd learned to control his baser impulses.

So he kissed her but restrained himself too.

Proud of his efforts, Conrad smiled into her lips, until he felt it . . .

Her hand.

On his cock.

He'd not even felt her reach beneath the coverlet, so busy he'd been congratulating himself on the small, fleeting victory.

How did she know . . .

She wrapped her hands around him before he could stop her. Cait's small, unsure hands were actually stroking him.

Nay, it could not be.

"Once"—she pulled away to whisper into his ear, although she continued to move her hands—"I snuck into the stables at night, defying my parents' orders to do otherwise. My mare was due to give birth, and I worried for her."

Ah, God. He squeezed his eyes shut, trying not to feel.

"Thankfully, I never saw them. My brother Rory's moans stopped me before I'd turned the corner. But I could hear his words easily. 'Yes,' he said. 'Wrap your hand around me like that. Up and down, love. That's right.'"

He really, really did not want to hear this.

"I fled, of course, and never spoke of it. But I didn't forget it, and after I overheard a few other conversations between Rory and Terric, between some of the maids . . ."

Her movements, coupled with Cait's breath tickling his ear and the knowledge that, if he reached down and pulled her atop him, she might very well lose her virginity tonight . . .

She was moving much too quickly. He would spill his seed if she continued.

Thinking to stop her, Conrad placed his hand over hers.

And then she kissed him again. Deeply.

His body took over, guiding her hand as he claimed her mouth. Her moan, coupled with their hands working together . . .

What am I doing?

Tearing her hand from him was as difficult as

sliding a sword into a man's flesh. Painful, but necessary.

He'd meant to pull away completely, but the sight of her stunned faced stopped him. He hauled her up with him, despite the height of the bed. Pulling Cait next to him, then atop him, the coverlet was now flung fully off.

She sat on his legs, looking down the length of him as if she'd never seen a man this way before, and he supposed she likely hadn't. The unbridled appreciation in her gaze did nothing to calm his desire for her as she stared directly at his cock.

"I've never . . ."

Conrad closed his eyes. Even though he knew they could not do this, not yet, he said, "Take off your shift, Cait."

He felt her moving, and then . . . stillness.

Opening his eyes, he cursed himself for a fool.

Cait Kennaugh sat above him, nude, as beautiful as a goddess. The need to touch her was as undeniable as his attraction to her.

And so he did.

His hands were everywhere at once. Rolling with her, Conrad landed on top. Encouraged by the sounds she made deep in her throat, he kissed her collarbone as his hands reached up to cover her breasts. He explored her body, both frantic and thorough.

Her hands, once tentative, did the same.

But when she reached behind him, softly touching his buttocks, Conrad made another vow. He'd not dishonor her, but by God, when the time came, he'd ensure Cait Kennaugh understood what they'd missed by not doing this sooner.

As much as he wanted to play with those beautiful breasts, he now had one goal in mind. And she didn't stop him until Conrad lifted one of her legs and positioned himself beneath her.

"What . . ."

He looked up then, the single candle thankfully still burning so she could see him. Conrad knew she trusted him, but a reminder was needed at this moment. He could have gone more gently, eased into this.

But he would not.

"Trust me, my sweet dove."

Her eyes widened.

He'd committed each of her letters to memory, and so he remembered it was in her fourth missive she'd told him of her affinity for the dovecote she managed at Bradon Moor. He'd first used the nickname in his fifth letter. It seemed fitting, Cait's love of the small yet powerful bird.

She understood. And did not flinch at the first touch of his tongue.

When her back arched a moment later, her hips pushing into him, Conrad smiled against her, glad for the pleasure he would give her, even as he denied his own release. It was pleasure enough to hear her moans, and when she called out his name, he refused to relent.

He could hear her hands grasping for something and imagined himself buried deep inside her, Cait's hands reaching for him. As they would be. Someday.

For now, he'd content himself with the cries that would surely wake the entire manor. The thought of gliding into that wetness, claiming Cait as his . . .

They could marry this moment. Say the words that would be as binding as any ceremony.

He will kill you. And you'd deserve it.

Instead, Conrad shifted his head to watch as Cait's expression changed from pleasure to pure wonder. The look she gave him then was worth the painful throbbing he endured at this moment.

Smiling, Conrad pushed his way up the bed and laid his head on the pillow next to hers. He closed his eyes. Calmed his breathing. Pretended to be on the battlefield, staring down mounted knights with lances at the ready. Any man who said he was fully prepared for such a sight lied.

Mock battle, the melee, was nothing akin to real men aiming to kill you.

"Conrad?"

Painful memories, but they had worked.

"I will need you to put on your shift, if you would stay here with me."

Cait did not hide her amusement. "Will you not dress as well?"

"I sleep nude. As you will when we are married."

They'd not spoken of it openly yet, and as Cait sat up and complied with his request, he found himself holding his breath as he awaited her response.

Covered finally, she turned toward him.

"I did not realize . . ."

It pleased him that she was at a lack for words.

"'Twas but a taste of the pleasures we will find to-gether," he said, pulling her back toward him. They moved into the now-familiar position of Cait tucked into him, and despite his longing, the need for her that had nearly killed him, Conrad was somehow able to find peace.

"I did not know," she repeated.

Conrad smiled against her neck. "'Twould not be the same with any other man."

He didn't know if she believed him or not, but Conrad spoke the truth. He'd been with other women, but love had never entered into any of those arrangements. It felt so different to touch Cait, to pleasure her. Which was why he prayed for strength. Knowing Cait, she'd not relent, even after this night. But if he had restrained himself with her hand on his . . . with the taste of her on his lips.

There was nothing she could do to convince him otherwise.

She would arrive in London a virgin.

And then, they would be married after he received Terric's blessing.

Aye, that is precisely how they would proceed.

CHAPTER 22

"Will the nuns think ill of us for sleeping in the same chamber?" Cait asked as they rode up to the abbey, darkness having fallen long ago.

Cait had discovered the greatest enjoyment of her life: teasing Conrad. Although she'd always enjoyed teasing her brothers, this was much, much more rewarding. He did not brood as her brother Terric did at times. Nor did he tease her back so mercilessly, like Rory, that she was forced to call for a truce.

Instead, he remained mostly silent, making Cait wonder at the effect of her words—and deeds—until he gave her one of his simple, intense looks of desire, which told her all she needed to know.

The men rode both ahead and behind them, leaving none to overhear their conversation. Torches from all around the abbey lit the sky ahead, a beautiful sight. Whitlock Abbey had once been a monastery. According to Conrad, it had been built more than five hundred years ago, and the Reverend Mother had been a friend to Licheford since before she served the Church.

"Sister Antonia will be told we are related. And that your chaperone took ill."

Cait covered her mouth in mock horror.

"You intend to lie to a woman of God? For shame, my lord."

Conrad scowled at her, or so she imagined. The waning moon offered little light to guide them. If not for the abbey, they'd have stopped long ago.

"Aye, and so will you. I'll not have her looking at you as the countess did. You have nothing to be ashamed of, but as you say, judgements will be made despite it."

"And yet, you can keep a mistress"—she'd been wanting to mention this before but had not found an appropriate time—"and none consider it shameful."

This time, Conrad had no retort.

This time, they both knew she was no longer jesting.

"'Twas the way of it, aye," he said finally. "Though I did tell her before I left."

They slowed, approaching the arched stone gateway of the abbey.

"What did you tell her?" she asked, afraid of the answer.

Conrad slowed to a stop.

When the men behind them caught up, Conrad nodded for them to ride ahead. He did not speak until the sound of their horses' hooves died down, leaving only the sounds of their horses' breathing and her own heartbeat.

"I thought you had remained behind," he finally said.

Not precisely an answer.

"What did you tell her?" she repeated.

* * *

HE'D TOLD her their relationship was over. That he would marry another.

Even then, Conrad had intended to make this Scotswoman his wife. And yet, he couldn't bring himself to tell her that he'd meant to forgive her, to embrace her, before learning the truth of why she'd pushed him away.

"Lord Licheford," one of the men called from the gates.

He would explain later.

Now, he needed to explain their situation to Sister Antonia to ensure they had beds for the night. Kicking his mount forward, Conrad joined the others, surprised to see the Reverend Mother herself standing at the door of the west range. He'd expected a cellarer to greet them at this hour. And she was not alone. A man had stepped up beside her.

Bishop Salerno?

Conrad didn't hide his surprise. Dismounting, he quickly walked to Cait and assisted her down, noting her narrow-eyed look of displeasure.

As their horses were led to the stables, Conrad approached the abbey and greeted them both, Cait beside him.

"Your Grace. Reverend Mother," he said with a bow, then stood. "Do you oft greet visitors here?" he asked, knowing the answer already.

He'd been here many times in the past with his father, so he knew the usual way of things.

"Only ones such as yourself."

But how could she have known they were coming?

"I jest, Licheford," she said with a small smile. "We were just walking the cloister when your men approached."

She glanced at Cait then, and Conrad introduced her as his cousin. If either she or the bishop found it odd that Cait should be traveling with him, sans a chaperone, neither said a word.

"It seems you've embroiled yourself quite deeply in the king's affairs?" the Reverend Mother asked.

Conrad was about to respond when the bishop interjected.

"While your guest settles for the evening," he said to Conrad, "I would speak with you privately." He pointed to the covered walkway, which was lined at intervals with several glowing lanterns. The cost of keeping them lit, likely every eve, must be staggering.

Conrad nodded, trying not to smile at Cait's foiled plans. For an innocent, she was surprisingly bold, and though he very much enjoyed every moment they were together, he feared each night may be the one he dishonored her. Conrad had thought the bond of friendship he'd forged with Terric, Lance, and Guy to be stronger than any other.

He loved those men above all others.

Until Cait.

He wanted to know her. All of her. The idea of it consumed his every waking thought, even in the midst of his present mission. Even now, as one of the most powerful men in the Church was asking to speak with him.

"Of course, Your Grace."

He took one final glance at Cait, confident she would be taken care of, and fell in step with one of the most important supporters of their cause.

"I am surprised to find you here," Conrad said, glancing at his companion in the dim light.

"Are you?"

An intelligent man, one whose history with the

king was as long and storied as his own, shoved his hands together beneath the long sleeves of his robes.

"So close to London," he speculated. "And so far from St. Christopher's."

"'Tis not an accident, Licheford."

"I was once Conrad to you."

Bishop Salerno stopped, and Conrad did the same.

"You are no young knight any longer. Nor are you just the son of a well-respected man. You are the leader of a rebellion against the Crown, an earl in your own right, and so Lord Licheford will do nicely, I believe. As such, you must also excuse the bluntness of what I am about to say."

This man had given the order enough coin to send a mercenary army back to France. One that could have, *would* have, fought for the king. Without him, their cause would have been lost last year.

So aye, Conrad would hold his gaze and listen to him with as much respect as he would have given his own father.

"I came to the same conclusion as you, which is why I am here, in the south. We've few enough resources to overcome John's supporters one by one. But if you take London peaceably, showing him popular support is with us, I believe he will be forced to negotiate."

So far, his words were not cause for concern. It was the very conclusion they had reached at Licheford, and the reason he was on his current mission. But the bishop knew all of that already. He was the kind of man who knew things before they happened.

"Aye," he agreed.

"If you fail in London, the rebellion is over."

"Perhaps. Taking London would certainly be

preferable. Though we lost the support of Lennox with the earl's death, Lindemere is sending men instead."

Understandably, Bishop Salerno's eyes widened.

"With his connection to France, the possibility of Louis's support . . . we should be in good standing. All twenty barons remain at the ready, thanks to Kennaugh's victory at Dromsley. He has sent men to London, along with Stanton and Noreham."

"I do not doubt you have the men necessary to claim victory."

John had no mercenary armies, and he'd lost crucial support from his barons over the winter months. Even now, he continued to increase taxes, something that angered men on both sides of the divide. Aye, it would be easier to bring about negotiations with John's treasured London under their control, but if that failed . . .

"You asked for my help once."

Conrad was well aware of it.

"And you gave it. For that, we are grateful."

"And why, exactly, did you come to me?"

He was confused. "We had not the funds to bribe Bande de Valeur to return to France. To convince them not to fight for John."

"Think on it, Licheford. You came to me because . . ."

"The Church has more money, more influence, than even the king himself."

He knew something. Salerno knew something Conrad did not.

"Guala Bicchieri is in England."

Conrad startled. "The pope's nuncio?"

"Aye, and his papal legate as well."

A chill crept up his back, and suddenly it felt like the inky darkness of night was closing in on them, even cloistered as they were in their well-lit pathway. This did not bode well.

"He moves quickly in the king's interest on behalf of the pope."

Conrad nearly cursed, catching himself at the last moment.

The pope only supported King John because he'd pledged himself to crusade. He manipulated Rome as surely as he did his own people.

"Already word spreads. It's said he intends to punish English clerics who support the rebellion, to remove them from their positions."

This was not welcome news. Conrad did not need to be told what would happen if Bicchieri were successful. Threatened in such a way, they would lose support from the Church.

"A few of us will stand against him still, but most"—Salerno frowned—"will not."

Conrad could feel his face getting warm, his hands forming fists at his sides. This would undo everything they had fought for. It might very well end the rebellion.

Taking a deep breath, reminding himself of how little his anger would accomplish, Conrad released his fingers from their firm grasp. He thought of the men likely already camped outside the city's walls. Of each of the pieces they'd put in place. And of their cause itself.

It was right. And just. And must prevail.

"It appears, Your Grace, that we must take London," he said, repeating Salerno's words. "And soon."

The bishop nodded. "May God be with you."

Conrad hoped he was, for luck certainly did not appear to be.

CHAPTER 23

Cait had planned to seek Conrad out, abbey or not, but by the time she was shown to her small stone bedchamber, she was eager to sit. To rest. She would undress, brush her hair, and prepare properly for bed. But first, just a wee rest.

When she awoke, it was to knocking at her door. The chamber she'd been given had neither a hearth nor windows, so when she saw Conrad there, it took her a moment to realize he was prepared for the day.

"What hour is it?" she asked, her backside still sore, a yawn escaping.

"Nearly sunrise."

It could not be.

"I . . . slept through the night?"

His eyes traveled up and down her person, giving Cait very unholy thoughts. A bell rang out just then, for vigils most likely.

"You did, my lady."

He seemed amused.

"And your wicked plans were foiled."

"Wicked?" She pretended to gasp. "I am the innocent here, if you will remember."

Though what he'd done to her the other night was

138

anything but innocent. A wicked vision popped into her thoughts of Conrad's eyes looking up at her from between her legs.

"Do not"—Conrad backed away as if she were a fire and he were afraid of a wee burn—"look at me that way. Not now."

Two of his men appeared just behind Conrad. "'Twill be easy for you to ready yourself," Conrad teased, gesturing to the clothes she'd slept in. "We shall meet below when you are ready. The horses have already been prepared."

That surprised her. "We will not break our fast here?"

It was then she noticed—Conrad looked worried.

"Something is amiss?"

Rather than answer her, Conrad bowed and backed away, joining his men. "I will explain on the road."

And then he was gone.

Cait stood at the door, willing him to come back. Even in her sleep she'd missed the familiar warmth of him. Already, she'd grown to rely on it. He had quickly become a part of her life Cait could not imagine living without.

As she prepared, Cait remembered the emptiness, the intense loneliness she'd felt after deciding not to continue their correspondence. After deciding she should free Conrad from his obligation to write her. If her mother had not pressed her to marry Colin, she'd not be here now.

Rushing outside to join him, Cait watched as he bid farewell to the bishop who had pulled him away last eve. He must be the cause of Conrad's concern. What had he told him? And where was the abbess? At vigils, most likely.

"Until we meet again, my lady."

Though she'd hardly spoken to the man, Bishop Salerno looked at her as if he knew her, as if he could see all the way down into her soul. Cait tried not to squirm under his scrutiny.

"You should marry," he said to her then.

So, Conrad had told him the truth?

"I . . ." Cait hardly knew what to say.

"Your Grace?"

The bishop gave Conrad his attention.

"'Tis unseemly to travel with an unmarried maid." Despite his words, the bishop did not sound judgmental. It was a statement of fact, and one they all knew to be true.

"Who are you?" he asked her.

Cait's pulse raced, but when Conrad nodded, she relaxed. The thought of directly lying to a man of God . . .

"I am Cait Kennaugh, sister to the chief of Clan Kennaugh and Earl of Dromsley."

If he was surprised, the bishop did not show it.

"How did you come to be with these men on such a dangerous mission?"

Again, Conrad nodded.

Her face beginning to flush, Cait searched for words that would not incriminate her. Failing to find any explanation save the truth, she said, "I've known the earl for many years through Terric. When he set out for London, I followed him. To convince him that we should marry."

Even that did not manage to shock the bishop.

"I could perform such a ceremony here. This morn."

"Aye!"

"Nay."

She and Conrad spoke at once. His objection,

however, was even more adamant than her assent. Both she and the bishop turned toward him.

"We have no time, as well you know. Rest assured, Cait Kennaugh will become my wife, but not without her brother's permission. But I thank you for praying for both of our souls and for the assistance you've given our cause." His voice firm, Conrad left no opening for either her or the bishop to argue.

Perhaps he really did not wish to marry her. He claimed he'd forgiven her, but Conrad's actions indicated otherwise. As he shook hands with the bishop, who gave her a polite nod in parting, Conrad had an expression she'd seen on Terric's face all too often.

His decision had been made, and he would not be swayed.

She mounted with Conrad's assistance but said nothing as they rode out of the abbey's courtyard. In fact, she said nothing for some time.

Cait could feel Conrad's gaze, though she refused to look at him to confirm it.

"The pope's nuncio is here in England to quash our rebellion."

She kept her gaze straight ahead.

"Bishop Salerno believes if we are not successful in London, we will have lost our chance to bring the king to heel. And I concur. Taking the city, showing John we have the majority's support, is our last move."

Cait knew she was being silly.

Of course they should not marry without speaking to Terric first. Besides which, Conrad had plenty of other issues on his mind. He was the leader of a rebellion against a king—one that was very much underway.

And yet she was still angry.

"Cait?"

She intended to tell him it was nothing, that she was merely tired, yet the angry part of her insisted otherwise. "You keep dismissing me out of hand. First in front of the countess, and again with the bishop."

"I am trying to protect you. To preserve your honor."

Cait made a sound that was distinctly unladylike. "Well, well. I thank you, my lord, for your steadfast support of my *honor*."

If she were being unreasonable, then so be it. She had no wish to discuss the matter with him further. Conrad must have realized it since he stopped attempting to get her to speak to him.

It was the longest morning yet. A steep incline coupled with gray skies that eventually opened just enough to dampen them, the weather making Cait's foul mood even worse. By the time they stopped for a midday meal, she was already sore, wet, and confused. Yesterday, she'd spent the day attempting to break down Conrad's final barriers. Today, she was more interested in sulking.

When Ansel produced bread, presumably from the abbey, she accepted it only because Cait knew she needed to eat. Even though the loaf had been freshly baked, it tasted like ash in her mouth.

It helped not at all that Conrad appeared completely unaffected by the current circumstances. Sitting as tall and proud as ever, the silver threads of his surcoat gleaming, he sat across from her on a flat rock, speaking to the men and not even glancing her way.

Which was just as well. She did not care if he failed to notice her. It was what she

wanted, was it not? He had more important matters to attend to than her, so let him do it. She would
sit here content to eat her bread in soggy silence.

CHAPTER 24

By the time they arrived at the Hart and Hound Inn, Conrad's mood was more foul than the innkeeper's breath. The drizzle that had begun the moment they'd ridden out that morn had yet to stop, as long-lasting as Cait's silence, and he could not shake the thought that the others had all likely arrived in London. He wanted nothing more than dry clothes, a mug of ale, and a meal.

Perhaps there was one thing he wanted more, but she was presently still ignoring him. He'd tried twice since that morn to engage her, but Cait seemed content to speak to every one of his men except him.

Married.

Did she really think Terric would allow him to live if they arrived in London as husband and wife? Guy may have found his bride at one abbey and wed her at the next, but Conrad could not do the same. Not when his bride's brother was the man who'd once knocked down so many men in a melee he'd been declared "the Scot," as if he were the only one that counted at the tournament.

Neither did Cait deserve such a wedding, a fact she did not seem to care about at the moment, judging by her frown. He'd secured private rooms for everyone in their party. It was the last night they would sleep with a roof overhead until they reached London, and even if the innkeeper refused to draw more than one bath, it was something of a luxury. The men seemed to appreciate it, though the frown Cait gave him as they were led toward the second floor indicated she did not currently appreciate anything about him.

At least she was looking at him now.

"This way, my lady." The serving girl motioned Cait toward one of the doors. "My lord has ordered a tub, which I will attend to forthwith. Will you take your meal in the room as well?"

"Aye," he answered for her. He could not abide the thought of Cait eating in the hall of an inn more likely to host smugglers than noblemen.

The answer appeared to anger her, causing Conrad even more confusion. He merely wished to keep her safe. But he had no time to explain himself, for Cait moved into the room without another word.

"And you, my lord?" the maid asked. "Will you take your meal up here as well?"

"I will send for it, and for my lady's meal, when it is required," he said by way of an answer.

The men all safely ensconced in their rooms, Conrad threw open the door of his own bedchamber, startling the maid. She scurried away, leaving him to find his way inside with the sole candle she'd given each of them on the way upstairs.

Like the great room and the hallway, the room was small and dark. Tossing his belongings to the side, Conrad began to undress. As they had all day, his thoughts flitted from London to the bishop and back Cait.

Always Cait.

No matter that they were in the midst of a rebellion.

I cannot do this.

The thought forced its way inside despite Conrad's attempt to push it away. Of course he could do this. The plans were well underway. His friends were likely already in position. He had dealt with each issue as it arose, the pope no more of a problem than any other.

He was the one who'd started all of this, and now they were taking on not just the king, but the pope as well. What had he been thinking?

He was not his father.

Shaking away the thought, Conrad found himself at the door before he even realized it. Pulling it open, he stepped out into the hall just as three serving girls left Cait's room with empty buckets of water.

He didn't pause to think. Rather, he pushed open the door and stepped inside just in time to watch her lift her shift above her head. She spun, startled, tugging the shift back down.

"I told you to lock the door at all times."

It wasn't how he'd intended to greet her.

Cait frowned.

"They just came in with the water," she said by way of explanation, nodding to the tub.

He locked it himself.

"What are you doing?"

Conrad would have thought it were obvious. "Undressing, of course. For the bath. They could only fill one."

Cait froze.

"Then I will allow you to bathe, my lord."

If she thought he was too gentlemanly to agree, Cait thought incorrectly. He tossed his clothing and boots to the side and entered the steaming hot water.

It felt good, though not as good as Cait would feel on top of him.

"Come here, Cait."

She shook her head. "Nay."

"Come here."

She did not move.

"I will ask you once more. And if you do not take off your shift and come to this tub, I will gather you myself. And your shift will be as wet as I intend to make you."

He meant every word. They could discuss her anger later. They could speak of marriage and his insistence on seeing to her safety. Of the state of the rebellion and his role in it and the fears he dare not express.

But right now, he needed her. Terric be damned.

"I am scared, Cait. I am alone and scared," he said, perhaps too honestly.

She took a step toward him.

CHAPTER 25

She had never seen him like this.

Nay, Cait corrected herself. She had seen a version of the man in the bath, but that had been many years ago. The look in his eyes now was much the same as it had been when he stared back at her, cheek oozing blood, willing her to be okay.

This was a man accustomed to having his orders followed. One who had been groomed to become an earl but who also harbored doubts.

I am scared, Cait. I am alone and scared.

Hard to believe Conrad was afraid of anything, but he had never told her an untruth, to her knowledge. Still angry but also aware that he needed her, she took the final step that put her within reach of him.

His tug on her hand was anything but gentle. She found herself, rather quickly, being pulled into the tub. Although large enough to accommodate a large man, as it likely often did, it was hardly big enough for them both. There was nowhere for her save directly on top of him. She straddled him, with Conrad's assistance, and he kissed her like they hadn't touched each other for the entire day, which they hadn't. Hard. Demanding. And that's when she felt his hand between her legs. She'd spent so much time thinking about his mouth on her, wishing it would happen again, that it took her a moment to decide if this was real or another fantasy.

Real.

Very, very real. She hardly had time to react before his fingers slipped inside. Just as before, a delicious pressure built inside her.

"Show me," she managed against his lips.

But he didn't respond. Instead, Conrad kissed her again, his hand moving against her even as her hips pressed into them. It was heaven. Pure heaven. A blasphemous thought, to be sure, but Cait could not be sorry for it. Nothing in her short life had ever felt so perfect. But if he thought to pleasure her again and not allow the same for himself . . .

"Show me," she said again, this time ensuring he understood her meaning. Cait found him easily, her hand wrapping around him as it had the other night, before he had stopped her.

Moaning, Conrad broke away. He looked into her eyes even as his fingers continued to taunt her. She remembered how he'd moved their hands together that night, showing her how to pleasure him, and she mimicked those movements now, staring into his eyes.

Cait was doing something right. His mouth opened, the look of pure pleasure on his face one she vowed to see every day of their lives.

"You should not."

His palm pressed against her, moving in slow, sensuous circles, as his fingers continued their delicious assault.

"That is enough." She was finished taking orders. "You do not speak for me. I am a grown woman and can speak and act for myself. I will do as I will, and if you think to stop me, then do it now so I know your measure. Otherwise, you will trust that I can make a decision all on my own. And just this moment . . ."

Just this moment, she was having difficulty remembering what she'd planned to say. His hand, his expressions . . . her own stroking of the evidence of his desire for her. It was simply too much.

"Just this moment, you will succumb to me," she finished on a gasp.

She could see the very moment he did.

Conrad thrust into her hand, shuddering. Letting go. And it was simply too much all at once. Her body split apart, Cait crying out his name as he did the same for her. She reached behind him and held on to the edge of the wooden tub, her entire body wracked with tremors she could not contain. He kissed her as the tremors of pleasure still ran through her, holding her as if he never wished to let her go.

Nor did she wish him to.

"What is it like to make love?" she asked, pulling away just enough to ask.

Conrad swallowed, his wet hands pushing back her hair on both sides as she allowed herself to fall atop him completely.

"With us, it will be all-consuming. It will feel as if you no longer live in the world, if just for a moment. The thought is almost frightening."

With us.

The implication that it would be different with them, better, made her heart soar. He'd said as much before, but she wouldn't tire of hearing it. They still had much to discuss, but for now, Cait wanted only to revel in the feel of his strong body under her. Of his hands, as gentle as he was hard, cupping her face as if she were a wee baby bird.

Just like that day.

The day they met, he'd both killed a man and looked at her with such softness Cait had thought he must be two different men.

But he was not.

He was simply Conrad.

And he was hers. Utterly and completely hers.

She leaned down to where the scar began, just near his ear, and kissed it. She kissed it all the way down his cheek, so gently that she could hardly feel her lips against his flesh.

At first Cait thought it was water from the bath. Until a warm drop fell onto the corner of her mouth just as she was sitting up again. Not water, but a tear.

Conrad was crying.

This knight, this earl, this brave man who'd taken the weight of England on his shoulders, was crying.

And that's when she understood the depth of his pain.

She had been hurting. His people, his country, were hurting.

He'd sought to heal them both.

And lost himself instead.

* * *

CONRAD PULLED CAIT AGAINST HIM, ruing the small bed but grateful to have one just the same. Her wet hair brushed against his chest as she settled next to him. Thankfully, her shift and his linen braies separated them.

Every time he thought of what it would feel like to finally slide into her, to be closer than they'd ever been before, Conrad imagined Terric asking, as he would, if he had taken her. Determined to answer, "nay," to repair the damage he had done by keeping his communication with Cait secret for so long, he resisted the urge to slip his hand under her shift. To bring her to pleasure again, to spend this night exploring every luscious curve.

"We must talk."

"Cait." He kissed the top of her head. "I would have married you today. Yesterday. Years ago. But we cannot do so without your brother's consent."

She stirred but remained quiet.

"You asked me not to tell him, and I never did. But the omission hurt him, and I'm sorry for it."

"You spoke for me."

She spun toward him, her face cradled in his arms. How small she looked this way.

"With the countess. The bishop. You spoke for me, as my father and brothers always have, but Terric does not do so with Roysa. She speaks for herself, as does Idalia. And I wish to do the same."

"I aim only to keep you safe."

"And with the bishop? Could you not have asked for my opinion before declining his offer?"

When he didn't answer, Cait rolled her eyes.

"Did your father ask for your mother's opinion on such matters?"

His answer was an easy one. "Nay."

"Never?"

"Not on matters of import."

He could tell she was getting upset again, but Conrad had simply answered the question honestly. And from what he knew of Cait's father, neither would he have consulted his wife.

"When you formed the order, did you ask for my brother's opinion? For Lance and Guy's? Or did you order them to join you?"

He thought back to that day at the tournament last year. He'd known what he was asking. None had hesitated to join him, but it had very much been their choice.

"They are free men. None are in my service. Of course I asked."

"Could you not ask me, at times? Rather than ordering me about as if I am in your service?"

"When your safety is not a concern, aye."

She seemed to contemplate that. Then finally, she said, "'Tis a bargain."

He'd not realized they were negotiating. Shaking his head, Conrad stared at her in awe. "You are a wonder to me, Cait Kennaugh."

"But I am *your* wonder, am I not?"

Of that, he was certain. "Aye."

Which was why he could not wait much longer to marry her. He knew the implications of what the bishop had told him—if they failed, the rebellion failed. All of them, but Conrad more than the rest. He'd started this movement, after all. The possibility that he would be taken, imprisoned, killed, was stronger than the outcome they prayed for—that the rebels would be welcomed, embraced, as champions of justice against a corrupt king.

He would not die without knowing her as fully and completely as a man and woman could. And so, they would marry before they entered the city.

Slipping away from her, Conrad jumped from the bed.

"What are you about?"

He didn't answer. Instead, he reached for the leather bag that carried his belongings. Pulling out an old slip of parchment folded into a small square, he returned to the bed. He handed it to Cait and watched as she opened it.

Her expression told him she'd understood at once. Propped on one arm, lying sideways, he could not resist smiling as she looked in astonishment from the letter back to him.

"How . . . but you, you did not know I had come when you brought this."

Conrad shook his head gently. "I did not."

"'Tis the very first one," she said.

Conrad waited.

"Did you look for this when I came to Licheford?"

Again, he shook his head.

"You carry it . . ."

"Always."

Cait's eyes filled with tears.

"You could not know I'd come. Lady Threston . . ." She took a deep breath as Conrad wiped a tear from her cheek. "You could not have known."

"I did not," he confirmed. "Neither did I believe I would ever see you again."

"But . . ." She looked down at the letter she'd sent him, the simple thank you note for helping the others to rescue her.

"'Twas a reminder of a time I had succeeded. A reminder," he continued, "of a woman I'd loved."

"You kept this with you?"

"Always," he repeated, taking it from her hands. "I love you, Cait. I wish to marry you the moment we meet up with the others."

"The moment?" She reached up, her hand covering his cheek. Conrad held his own over it.

"The moment. Before we go to London."

Before we either force the king's hand or die trying.

"Yes. Yes!"

She sat up and kissed him in a way that made Conrad rethink his position with Terric. Her lips moved across his own so sweetly and thoroughly, Conrad wondered if the entire plan could not be altered. If they could, all eight of them, forget London.

And King John. Escape to France, or anywhere really, and find peace without the need for war.

But even as he held the woman he'd never quite forgotten, positioning himself for sleep behind her, breathing in her sweet scent, he dismissed the wild notion. Guy and Sabine could escape. Idalia and Lance too. Even Terric could flee across the border to Scotland, never to return to England again.

But Conrad had begun this rebellion. He would see it through.

Whatever the outcome.

CHAPTER 26

"Oh dear."

As the outer walls of Heath Castle came into view, Cait's bravado of the past few days began to wane. Although the castle itself was most impressive, it wasn't the structure or its proximity to London that gave her pause.

Bright white tents littered the landscape for as far as she could see. Not even the battle at Dromsley Castle had prepared her for this sight.

"There must be . . ."

She could not guess.

"Over a thousand men," Conrad finished for her. "And more are striking southward toward the Sussex coast. We're prepared to seize a port where our foreign allies may land."

She slowed, her hands shaking.

"Conrad . . ."

It had not precisely felt real until this moment. She'd only seen this many knights and warriors in one place on one previous occasion.

And that had not ended well. Not at all.

"We have been preparing for this for a long time," Conrad said softly, his tone encouraging. "All has gone according to plan."

It wasn't true, of course—neither of them had forgotten about the bishop's disclosure. Her father and brother had regularly downplayed the danger of their missions, something she and her mother had bemoaned together.

But if it allowed Conrad some measure of peace, to imagine she believed all would be well, then she'd not chastise him for it.

"I know you have," she said, reassuring him more than herself. "But . . ."

Though the dirt road on which they traveled remained clear, they were surrounded by the clashing of swords and shouting of commands. It was impossible to forget what had brought them here.

And then it began.

A low murmur at first, Cait not understanding what was happening.

It became louder and louder, the chant clearer with each step forward. Could it be? Did her ears deceive her?

When Conrad raised his fist in the air, a cry went up that nearly unseated her.

"Licheford!"

They were calling *his* name.

And why not?

Conrad and a few important rebels had made this happen. She looked over at him again, attempting to reconcile the man, chin raised, jaw locked, with the one whose arms she'd slept in these past nights.

She could not do it.

"Licheford!" they cried, the name echoing into the early evening sky. Cait shuddered as the drawbridge was lowered for them.

Lord Sarnac, former constable of the Tower of London and one of the order's earliest supporters, greeted them just inside the gates. At least, she assumed the man sitting atop one of the largest destriers she had ever seen was their host.

She shuddered again.

Conrad had described the lord of Heath Castle to her, but the man looked much more ferocious in person, his long, dark hair as straight as his horse's mane.

Thankfully, he appeared to be alone.

No Terric yet.

"They greet you properly," Sarnac said as they approached. "As I am wont to do for the man who set this upon our heads." He gestured back outside the gates from which they'd just entered. "Welcome to Heath Castle."

Their host shifted toward her.

"Greetings, Lady Cait. And welcome."

She answered in kind, startled he knew her name. Which meant . . .

"So they are here?" Conrad asked.

"Aye, just inside the keep. Though I wish I could give you a better greeting, I am actually preparing for a ride among the men. But my squire here will lead you inside."

Ah, so the mount was a show of force for those who would soon be following him into battle.

"Many thanks, Lord Sarnac. For your welcome. And your hospitality."

Just then two men on horseback rode up to their lord, prepared to flank him, no doubt.

"Arnie, see to our guests, lad."

The boy next to Sarnac nodded to them, then kicked his mount and turned toward the inner gatehouse. With a final farewell, their host headed out just as she, Conrad, and the boy made their way inside. By the time they made it up the stone steps of the keep, Cait's heart-beat had nearly returned to normal—until the maid who'd greeted them asked if they would prefer to be "seen to their rooms, or to the hall with the others."

The others.

Meaning her brother.

"The . . ." Conrad stopped, gesturing for her to answer. Cait's entire body warmed as she realized why he failed to respond.

"The hall, if you please," she said. Part of her wished to put the confrontation off indefinitely, yet she also wished to get it out of the way.

"My lord will return before the evening meal," the maid said, leading the way.

Neither she nor Conrad corrected her assumption that they had not yet been greeted by Lord Sarnac. Did Conrad feel as nervous as she did? Likely not.

They'd been spotted.

She could not tell from whom the shriek originated, but there, in the corner of the hall, sat all of them. With the exception of Roysa, who was nearly running toward them. The others stood, the hall mostly empty with the exception of servants beginning to move the tables toward the center of the room for the midday meal.

Roysa rushed right past Conrad to wrap Cait in a hug. She squeezed the other woman back, grateful for such a welcome.

"We've been expecting you."

She glanced over her sister-in-law's shoulder and caught Terric's gaze. As expected, he did not appear very pleased.

"Is he angry?"

Roysa twisted her mouth, as she often did, but

gave no other answer. Which meant, aye, he was angry, but she did not wish to say it aloud.

"With me, I hope, and not Conrad," she whispered as Conrad walked toward the rest of the group.

They sat next to a fireplace that crept up the entire wall. Intricate carvings began close to the floor. The stonework was as fine as any Cait had ever seen. She spied a dragon, two actually, one on each side.

"He is better . . . now," Roysa whispered.

Cait didn't have time to ask about that before she was engulfed in another hug, this time by Idalia and then Sabine. The somber mood that had consumed her began to lift, despite the circumstances. Namely, her brother, and his likely disapproval of her presence here.

"I'd have a word with you both," he said, his voice booming as he approached them.

"Terric, they've just returned," Roysa interjected. "Are likely tired and hungry . . ."

"I am both," she acknowledged, catching Conrad's eye. "But I would speak to you now."

Before she even finished, Cait found herself enveloped in her brother's strong arms.

"I've not survived the journey for you to squeeze the life from me," she teased. Despite her words, Cait returned her brother's embrace. "I love you too," she whispered, feeling his urgency—his need to know she was, indeed, well.

He let her go finally, turning toward the front of the hall, which had begun to fill during their reunion. With one last glance at the women who had helped her "escape" Licheford, Cait followed Terric just as Conrad, who'd been greeting Lance and Guy, reached her side. Though he did not look her way, his hand found hers, his fingers winding through her own.

For a simple gesture, it was telling—Terric knew it too, judging by the frown he gave them as he directed them to follow him into a small chamber just off the hall.

"Sarnac has given use of his solar for our purposes," he said, leading the way inside. The dark interior began to illuminate as the wall torch Terric had grabbed just outside the door was used to light similar ones inside. The walls flickered with light, coming alive.

Sadly.

She could have lived a hundred years without seeing her brother's scowl. It was one she knew well, having seen it many, many times before.

"Again, Cait? After you stowed away with Rory, I did hope you'd learned your lesson."

"Terric." Conrad never let go of her hand. "I was angry as well. And considered sending her back."

"Considered. 'Twould seem a fine plan to me."

She hated seeing them this way. At odds, because of her. "Speak to me, Terric. Not him. I was the one who left. I am your sister and can accept your anger as I know it will pass. But Conrad—"

"Is my brother." Terric looked at their joined hands. "He has been so for many years," he added, his voice thick, "but it seems our bond will only grow stronger."

Cait had expected to beg and plead for her brother to be reasonable. She'd prepared many arguments. That his wife was here too. As was Idalia. That she was his elder. That he'd called Conrad the most honorable man he had ever known.

But it seemed none of the arguments were needed.

"Roysa and the others explained. Everything."

When Conrad squeezed her hand, Cait thought

she might cry. Terric's approval was the last barrier to a story that had begun years ago. She hadn't dared hope it would be this easy.

"I wish you had told me," Terric said to her, "but understand why you did not. Although I cannot pretend to understand why you hesitated to come to Dromsley for so long, avoiding a man you clearly love."

Cait rubbed her thumb along Conrad's hand.

"I avoided him because I was scared," she admitted.

And was even more so now to admit to the part she'd played in that awful, cruel day the brotherhood had been born. But it needed to be done.

"I asked him to meet me that day at the tournament."

"Cait . . . ," Conrad warned.

She ignored him.

"There was an instant connection between us. And as improper as it seems now, I felt bold that day. It was my first tourney. My first time away from home. The first time my entire body came alive at the mere sight of someone . . . and so I asked him to meet me. Alone."

Before Terric could react, she continued. "You and Rory were always with me. And when you competed, father stood guard, never allowing me more than a moment alone. So, I asked him to meet me," Cait repeated.

Her brother looked at Conrad.

"He refused. Said it was too dangerous."

Clearly Terric was confused, and she did not blame him.

"But I went anyway. I pretended to need privacy but ran all the way to the river behind the tents."

"I saw her go," Conrad finished. "And sought to

follow her. Rory stopped me. I could never remember what he asked, or what we spoke about, but you came along then."

"And asked you to walk with me," Terric finished.

He nodded. "I didn't want Cait to be down there alone, but I couldn't say anything without getting her in trouble. I planned to feign surprise when we saw her."

The room went silent, each of them remembering their version of what happened next. She'd planned to take off her boots, dip her toes in the river, enjoy the bit of freedom she'd managed to gain.

The man had grabbed her before she even saw him coming.

"It was my fault," she said, choking out the words like they were acrid smoke. Before Conrad could argue with her, she added, "But I know, now, it was actually more my attacker's fault than anyone's."

Another squeeze.

"I love her," Conrad said, his voice unwavering.

I will not cry. I will not cry.

"I fell in love with your sister when we corresponded and she told me of all her exploits, some you likely wish I didn't know." Conrad grinned at her brother. "And I love her even more now. I would marry Cait, with your permission, Terric."

When her brother smiled at his friend, Cait's silent plea was answered. Her eyes blurred.

"I give it gladly if you'll answer just one more question."

Cait's heart leapt in anticipation of what her brother might ask.

"Did you consummate the marriage you've yet to have?"

Her mouth dropped open. "Terric!"

"I know you well, my friend, and believe you have not. But Guy and Idalia do not agree."

"You . . ." She had no words. "You all speculated on whether or not we . . . Conrad and I. Terric!"

For his part, Conrad grinned broadly.

"We did not," he said, clearly proud of the fact. "But know this," he said over her brother's laughter. "We wed immediately. Before London. I'd hoped to give Cait a better wedding but . . ."

Terric crossed his arms, nodding his approval.

"Go ahead, then. Say the words."

This could not be happening. Did he mean . . .

Conrad spun her toward him, taking both of her hands.

Cait was about to be wed.

CHAPTER 27

"Tonight, we forget about the rebellion," Conrad whispered to his wife.

Freshly dressed, newly married, they sat beside each other on Sarnac's raised dais, honored guests. Even so, he'd arranged to be seated at the very end of the table, not wishing to share Cait with the others just yet. He snagged a morsel of meat from their shared trencher.

"Tonight," he said, just before placing it in his mouth, "we celebrate."

Conrad had never been happier in his life.

At first he'd thought Terric was jesting about marrying them, but the look in his eyes had assured him his friend was quite serious. There was trust and respect in his gaze, and a fair measure of *you will marry my sister after being alone with her*, which he'd expected. He had known it from the moment he'd chosen not to force her back to Licheford.

She might deserve a better man, or at least one who was not about to risk his life, but Conrad could no sooner stay away from Cait for a single night more than he could call off the whole rebellion. The torture of holding her, pleasuring her, without full consummation . . .

The memory of Cait's hand wrapped around him made him hard even now, sitting in the hall, with hundreds of men and a few women staring up at them.

He'd have given her a grand wedding, if he'd been able.

But Conrad vowed, at least, to give her the wedding night she deserved.

"Husband."

He finished chewing, the spiced meat tender but not so delicious as his wife's expression.

"I enjoy saying it."

Conrad's response was cut short by their host, who pounded the table with his mug to quiet the hall.

"A toast to the new bride and groom! To the man who brought us all together and the one who will lead us through the gates of Aldgate three days hence."

He would not celebrate that feat prematurely, but Conrad did raise his mug in deference to the woman he now called wife. She beamed, her smile as radiant as the sun.

The audience's cheers and banging mugs did not appear to be ceasing. The sound echoed through the hall, louder and louder until Conrad leaned over to Cait.

"Kiss me."

She didn't hesitate.

His wife leaned up to him, and Conrad kissed her so thoroughly Terric finally shouted, "Enough, 'tis my sister!" next to her. The crowd laughed, and drank some more.

Taking advantage of the jovial mood, Conrad stood, unwilling to wait a moment longer. Cait joined him, and as he'd expected, the crowd roared. Guy and Lance, along with their wives, smiled as he took Cait's hand and led her from the hall. His gaze lingered longest on Terric, who was laughing, a sound Conrad had sorely missed.

He didn't let go of Cait until they reached their chamber. Not his. Nor hers. *Theirs.*

Smiling at her, Conrad slowly opened the door.

He had been explicit earlier in his request to Sarnac. The man had done much for the movement —his agreement to host the forces likely placed him second on the monarch's list of rebel barons—and yet he had come through again.

The quite ordinary room he'd occupied for a bath earlier had been transformed, filled with deep pink camellias mixed with crocuses the color of Cait's kirtle.

"'Tis beautiful," she said softly.

Candles sat in every crevice of the chamber, and the fire had recently been stoked. Silently thanking his host once again, Conrad wasted no time. Gathering Cait in his arms, he murmured his agreement.

The kiss, as sweet as the one he'd given her in the hall, quickly became much more. He'd had a taste, but now Conrad wanted it all. Reaching behind her, he deftly unlaced the back of her gown, his fingers actually trembling. That day at the tournament, when she'd asked him to "meet me briefly by the river," he'd little thought the beautiful, timid, and bold young woman would one day become his wife.

Unlaced, he gathered both sides of her gown in his hands and lifted it above her head. Cait's shift was next to go. As she reached down then to untie the laces on her boots, Conrad focused on ridding himself of his own clothing, knowing their night might be over before it started were he to look upon his wife's breasts as she stripped off her stockings.

Slowly, Conrad.

Taking off everything but his shirt, he was about to divest himself of that as well when Cait stopped him.

"Nay," she said, pulling him toward her by that very garment. "Let me."

Except she did not move to take off his shirt. Instead, she leaned up to kiss him, and the sweet pressure of her lips made him lose patience. He needed her. Now. He picked her up, intending to take her to the bed, but when she shivered, he carried her to the fire instead. Placing her on the large fur pelt in front of it, he sat down beside her. Cait stretched herself out.

"Mmmm."

He was content to watch her, if only for a moment, as the firelight cast a shadow over the very part of her he intended to touch first. And so he did. Running his finger from her knee to her inner thigh, Conrad never took his eyes from her.

"You will be mine tonight," he said, aware of the gruffness in his voice.

"I am yours already." Cait bent her knee, so he took advantage and captured her leg.

"You are my wife, aye."

He splayed his hand across her thigh just before reaching his goal.

"But after this eve." Conrad inched closer. "There will be no question of the validity of our vows."

Her lips parted as he slipped one finger inside.

So wet, so ready.

"Your shirt," she said, her hips pushing into him.

Conrad laughed. "It seems you forgot to remove it."

He wanted to lean down and kiss her. To mimic the movement of his fingers with his tongue, to taste her as she came into his hand. But he also wanted to *see* Cait. To watch his wife as her breathing became deeper, more erratic. As her cheeks flushed from an internal heat that had naught to do with the fire that raged next to them.

"I did," she breathed.

Pressing his palm into her, moving it in circles, he could see she was close.

While he'd fully intended to watch her come apart in his hands, it had been too long.

He'd spent too many sleepless nights dreaming of her beneath him. Of sinking into her as he intended to do just now.

Tearing off his linen shirt, Conrad positioned himself over her and claimed her lips, his tongue delving into her mouth. The exquisite press of Cait's breasts against his chest threatened to drive him mad, but he forced himself to lift up.

He wanted them in his hands.

Conrad could not get enough of her. He propped himself up with one hand, using the other to explore her body. She pulled him back down, insistent, and he reached between them to position himself.

Ah, he was there. Right there.

Somehow he managed to rip his mouth from hers. "Cait?"

She knew enough to understand. Nodding, Cait squeezed her eyes shut.

He wasn't in the habit of bedding virgins and had little experience here, but he did know it would hurt some. But it was for him to soothe her afterward.

Little by little, he guided himself in, moaning for the sweet torture of it all.

There. The barrier that he'd refused to cross on

the hellish journey south. Knowing she wanted this as much as he . . .

Conrad stopped thinking. In one swift movement, he crossed the barrier and captured her cries with his mouth. Not moving, forcing her attention to the tangling of their tongues, Conrad waited for what seemed like forever.

Until she moved.

A little at first. Testing.

And then a bit harder. Her hips pressed upward, and so he circled her. Not daring to go too quickly.

"More," she said, breaking contact.

He had so much more to give.

Wanting to both close his eyes for the pleasure of being inside Cait and keep them open to watch her face, Conrad decided on the latter. Lifting her leg on one side, he sank in so deeply that for a moment he thought he'd hurt her again.

But her cry was of pleasure, not pain.

So he moved faster. Pumped harder.

Cait's nails dug into his back, and he welcomed them as a reminder of their union. If she left a mark, it wouldn't be the first he'd gain because of this woman. And like the first, he would revel in the reminder that they were linked.

Always.

"More." She met his every thrust, as if her virgin's barrier were a distant memory. His arse clenched in anticipation, her breathing and frantic moans telling him it would not be much longer. A pity, in some ways. But he'd wanted her too much, and for too long, for him to achieve the endurance he would have desired.

He couldn't hold out much longer.

"Conrad," she yelled, and he responded. With a final thrust, he cried out as she clenched against him.

The pressure was more than he could take as every muscle in his body tensed and then slowly, blessedly, relaxed.

Still joined, he pulled her on top of him, where his wife promptly collapsed.

Lying beside the fire, covered by his beautiful, spirited wife, Conrad could die a contented man.

Shoving aside the thought that he very well might die, and soon, he lifted Cait's head and laughed at her expression.

"Why," she said, pulling a strand of her hair behind her ear, "did you not do that sooner?"

He pulled out gently, repositioning them.

"You know the reason very well, lass."

She shook her head vigorously. "But if I'd known . . ."

Her entire body shivered.

Conrad could not stop smiling.

"'Twas the most difficult thing I've ever done, restraining myself these past days."

"The most difficult? Of all the things you have done? I do not believe you."

He could feel himself stirring already. Not unexpected given their position.

"Nay, 'twas not *the* most difficult."

Satisfied by his admission, she made a sound in the back of her throat. It reminded him of a kitten, but Cait was no mewling kitten.

She was more like a full-grown cat, one who could as easily hiss away its enemies as it could curl into a ball on your lap.

He did not want to dampen the mood, but he also would not lie to her. For too long they'd held back, and it had nearly kept them apart forever.

"The most difficult was to watch you ride away

from that tourney between your brothers, not knowing if I would ever see you again."

She tsked. "You hardly knew me."

"I knew enough."

Her smile faltered.

"We were meant to be together Cait," he said seriously. "I was meant to be there that day, to save you. And you were meant to come back into my life, to save me."

"But . . . I did nothing. I didn't save you at all."

"I had nothing. This rebellion . . ." He kissed her lips, just to reassure himself he still could. "Only a fool would be so daring. One who had little to live for but the approval of his people."

"And his friends."

"Aye," he agreed. "And them." He reached up to cup her cheeks. "But I have you now, Cait. And I vow to do everything possible to come back to you."

"You had best do so," she said, her expression both desperate and hopeful. "I did not make the journey from Bradon Moor, endure an attack at Dromsley, and disguise myself as one of your men just to become a widow."

"For that reason, we will persevere."

Any remaining doubts he had vanished.

He would not fail England.

He would not fail Cait.

Conrad was ready.

But first he'd make love to his wife. Again.

CHAPTER 28

Three days simply wasn't long enough.

The days had been spent strategizing, the nights with his friends, at supper, and then alone with his wife. After that first frenzied night, he had taken more time to learn every curve of Cait's body.

To relish the quiet moments just before they slept.

And to wake before dawn with her in his arms, watching her sleep for a few moments before dressing for the day. It had quickly become one of his favorite rituals, no less so for the knowledge that they had so little time before the maneuver.

That morning, their last, was even more bitter-sweet than the others. He soaked in the sight of her, the hair feathering her cheek, and stood from the bed.

"You would leave without saying goodbye," she murmured. Conrad sat back down, the feather mattress sinking under his weight.

"I didn't want to wake you." He kissed her forehead. "And we did say goodbye last eve."

Cait blinked away her sleep, opening her eyes fully.

"We did but . . ."

But they both knew there was a strong possibility he'd not return. They'd not spoken of the order's plans in detail, but Cait knew enough.

"I will return to you."

He said it with as much confidence as possible, knowing he would die trying to make it so. When she closed her eyes just briefly, Conrad lay his hand on her delicate cheek.

"Sleep, my dove."

Unable to look at her any longer, not knowing when, or if, he would return, Conrad left the bedchamber to find the others, her final whispered parting, "Adieu," still ringing in his ears. Only Guy appeared as cheerful as ever as he accepted a bundle from Lord Sarnac's squire.

The sun had not yet risen, but the courtyard brimmed with activity.

"I do not understand," Guy said. "Cait is quite a woman," he mocked, "but you dote on her in a way I would not have expected from you." Laughing at his own jest, or what Conrad supposed to be a jest, Guy mounted. His next comment was for Terric. "We've called ourselves brothers, but now the three of you are brothers in truth."

By marriage, both Conrad and Lance could now call Terric brother-in-law.

"If only I had another sister," Terric said, "or Stanton another daughter."

Guy winked at him, and Conrad rolled his eyes. "I would dearly love to say the same, but I love my wife more."

"You are our brother regardless," Lance said. The rest of them offered their agreement.

"All appears to be ready," Conrad said.

For as far as he could see, mounted men filled the courtyard. Sarnac would be outside the gates by now. He'd requested to lead with Conrad at the back.

"Aye." Terric was the last to be prepared, and when he was finally ready, he nodded to Guy, who would ride in the middle with him. "To Aldgate."

"To Aldgate," they all repeated, Conrad staying back with Lance.

Although they did not expect trouble on the two-day ride, their group numbered at over five hundred men, and it would be a slow slog with so great a party. Alone, Conrad could have made it there by dark. Instead, they would camp for the night at Renwith and then arrive outside the city's gates by nightfall the following evening.

"The noise," Lance said as they waited for the others to ride ahead. "'Tis what surprises me most."

As strong and fierce as any of them, Lance was the only one who had not been raised as a knight. His training had been with a blacksmith's hammer, not a broadsword. And though he had learned to wield one in their time together, this would only be his second battle.

The first had been at Dromsley Castle.

"It is as many men as I've ridden with as well," Conrad admitted. "Of the four of us, only Guy would have seen forces of this size."

Guy had fought in more than one mercenary company, at times with Bande de Valeur and others in France. He'd once told them a tale of him and his father fighting alongside the French king. It had been his closest brush with death, a festering wound that had unfortunately not convinced him of the merits of heavier armor.

Nearly always serious, Lance seemed even more

so now. Conrad understood, of course. What they were about to do . . .

"We will return."

He said it as much for himself as his friend.

"What do you believe he was thinking, your father, when he rode toward Westminster Hall?"

Conrad thought differently now than he had, having met Lindemere, a man who had nothing to gain for telling him anything but the truth.

"That he was in the right."

"As are we, my friend."

The certainty with which Lance spoke lit a flame inside of him. He admired his friend's grit, his steadfastness. Unlike Conrad, Lance had earned every single accomplishment—none had been given to him.

"Aye," Conrad agreed. "As are we."

If justice chose sides, they would surely win. But he feared history did not bear that out. Sometimes, little thieves were hanged while great ones escaped.

* * *

"Do we have the men to take it by force?"

"Are we prepared to lose them?"

An argument had broken out among the order and other leaders and continued throughout the morn. A letter had arrived at their camp, as expected, from inside London's gates. The news it contained, however, was not what they had hoped to hear.

They'd arranged for FitzWalter, the castellan of London and chief banneret of the city, to alert them when it was safe to enter. Key merchants, nobles, and laymen had assured FitzWalter there would be little resistance to the Order of the Broken Blade and its supporters. They would enter through Aldgate, which was to be conveniently left open while mass was being offered throughout the city.

Instead, the mayor of London wrote only, "Await the banner."

They watched from their position at the top of the ridge, all eleven officers of the rebellion staring at the banner. King John's three golden lions on a field of red waved in the wind from Aldgate's towers, jaunty and proud. No one seemed in a hurry to change or remove it.

"We cannot take London by force," Lord Noreham said once again. Some of the others disagreed with him. They'd carried on this conversation for some time, watching that infuriating banner. Conrad had thus far kept his silence, content to listen to the arguments on both sides, but the others had insisted he should make the final decision. He would lead them to victory, or to their final stand against the corrupt king.

Each of the men looked to him now.

They could wait until the conditions were ideal, until the few who opposed them were distracted. If they could enter the city walls peaceably, their numbers would easily overwhelm those who stood against them. And though they had brought enough men to take London by force, many would lose their lives, and victory was anything but guaranteed.

With the news he'd learned from Bishop Salerno .
. .

Conrad exchanged a glance with Terric.

His father had taught him to lead. Leading was often a lonely proposition, though, and his friends, the Order of the Broken Blade, had taught him the importance of not standing alone. He'd not make a rash decision. Taking a deep breath, Conrad glanced at the banner once more, still waving in the wind.

"We will lose support without the clergy. We will not have another chance."

Terric's nod was so slight, none other would have caught it. Aye, this was the right decision. Even if it cost some of them their lives.

"We take London," Conrad pronounced loudly enough for all men to hear.

For the briefest of moments, none of them spoke, and Conrad could hear the noise Lance had spoken of, the murmur of several hundred men outside of their tents.

In the next, everyone began talking at once. Everyone except for Guy.

It was so unlike him to remain silent at such a pivotal time that Conrad moved his position to stand next to the mercenary.

"Do you not agree?"

The sullen look on his friend's face reminded him of something he'd nearly forgotten in the chaos of the morning. Two nights prior, a messenger had arrived from Lord Brefton, who had been camped outside the city for more than a sennight.

A mercenary company had contacted him with an offer of assistance—a rarity given they did not typically concern themselves with politics. The messenger had refused to explain the reason for the offer but had said his master was none other than Bernard Lavallais.

Guy's father.

Unfortunately, though he'd sent the company, his father had not accompanied the mercenaries.

"Do we need them?"

He knew the answer Guy sought, but Conrad could not give it.

"If we move forward with an attack, aye, we will need every man willing to fight for us."

Guy's normally jovial mood, already soured by the persistent banner, did not improve with the knowledge that he would be forced to fight alongside men sent by a father who Guy did not wish to be indebted to.

"They are here because of you," he told Guy.

Conrad highly doubted the mercenaries cared about their cause. Or any cause. Coin was their usual motivation, and none was being offered here. Guy's father had only sent help because of Guy's involvement in the order.

"Any man who can convince a company of mercenaries to fight without payment does so out of love, however misplaced it might seem."

"Love," Guy scoffed. "Who is the man who stands before me?" He made to rejoin the others, all of whom were still loudly debating—although not refuting Conrad's decision.

"One who has likely just sentenced us to death," Conrad answered. "No invading force has taken London before without heavy consequence. And if we're captured . . ."

They would be coming for Conrad first.

The others quieted, looking at him, but he had only the truth to give them.

"It appears London does not welcome us. As you know, the task ahead is all but insurmountable. But if we go home now, we forfeit all to the king. Some more than others, for he will surely seize every title and bit of land and property we possess. If we fight, 'twill not be an easily won victory, but at least we will have tried."

He made sure all of them understood his decision. Satisfied, Conrad looked down at the banner once more. Still Lackland's.

He pictured Cait then, lying atop him on their

wedding night. He'd been right to insist on marrying her straightaway. Never had he possessed such a powerful motivation to fight. To win.

Conrad swallowed and then bellowed, "Who among you fights with me?"

CHAPTER 29

"I is so quiet."

Sabine said what all four of them were thinking.

At least, Cait had been. They sat in a stranger's hall, among servants they did not know. But they were, at least, safe. Meanwhile, Conrad and her brother were out there risking their lives. Cait shuddered.

"We must eat." Idalia picked up her pewter spoon, earning a smile from the steward who watched them from the side of the hall. A few men had remained to garrison the castle, but it felt so indescribably empty compared to how it had been just a few days past. Her family's hall in Scotland had felt much the same way after her father died.

Few spoke.

Even fewer smiled or laughed, for there was little cause to celebrate. They all knew what the bishop's revelations meant. This campaign was their very last stand against the English king. If they failed to take the king to task now, it would not happen, and all of the rebels would be punished.

"What do you believe is happening now?" Cait asked, not for the first time since the men left.

Roysa looked up to the ceiling, counting on her fingers. "I believe they have taken London."

Cait nodded firmly, wanting to believe it. "Aye. I believe that is where they are this very moment."

Sabine lifted her goblet, smiling at them with forced cheer. "To London. And to the rebellion. My parents would be proud."

All four lifted their goblets, the other women lifting her spirits, just slightly. She drank, wanting to ask again. How could they be sure? What if the men were not in London? What if they'd been forced to fight? Or worse, what if they'd been captured?

She stopped herself.

It was those precise thoughts that had kept her in Bradon Moor for so long.

What if Terric learned what she'd done? What if Conrad changed his mind about her? What if he reminded her of the trauma she had endured?

Nay, Cait would not allow herself to linger on what-ifs. She'd done enough of that for a lifetime.

"They will be victorious," she said, her voice firm. "They will be victorious and your king will be forced to negotiate with them."

All three women looked at her.

"Our king?" Idalia asked, smiling.

The comment caught her off guard, but Idalia was correct, of course. When they were successful. When Conrad returned. When this rebellion was over, they would reside at Licheford. After a visit to Bradon Moor, of course. Cait tried not to think of what her mother would say about it all.

Cait nodded. "I suppose you are right. Though I cannot be proud of the fact."

Roysa made a face. "If only we could all go north,

across the border. To be ruled by a worthier monarch. As you were."

Were. A strange thought, to no longer be a daughter of Scotland. In residence, at least. In Cait's heart, she would always be a Scotswoman first.

She'd been hesitant to ask before, but it seemed an appropriate question now.

"What of you, Roysa? Have you spoken to Terric about what will happen when this is all over?"

All eyes turned to her sister-in-law.

"'Tis as uncertain as the king's response when they do take London."

Cait knew better than the others what she meant.

The matter was complicated. Although Terric had been born mere minutes before Rory, he had inherited both the Scottish and English titles from their father. Despite Rory's pleading, Terric refused to relinquish either to him.

And Cait did not blame him for his hesitance.

Rory believed he was ready for such a responsibility, but his actions did not support such a claim. He still cared for his own pleasure more than his duties. Managing two such large properties was a challenge, and Terric would dearly love to bequeath either title on his brother, but Rory was just not ready.

"Do his clansmen resent him spending so much time in England?" Idalia asked her sister. "And bringing warriors to Dromsley?"

Roysa looked to Cait for the answer, as she had not yet been to Bradon Moor.

"'Tis a complicated matter," she admitted. "People outside of our clan don't understand it. But those who love my mother, and there are many, understand why Terric has joined the fight. The English king"—she frowned—"*our* king and his father have wronged her in many ways."

These women knew her parents' past, and hers. They knew the English king's role in her mother's inheritance being taken away. They knew one of his closest advisors had attempted to rape her. None questioned her clan's loyalty. "Others, of course, believe Terric's duty is to Clan Kennaugh. And not to Dromsley. They think he should be back in Scotland."

Roysa reached for her sister's hand. "As for what happens after this is over, I'm not yet sure, but Bradon Moor is just across the border. And you"— she shifted her gaze to Cait, then Sabine—"all of you will only be a few days' ride away. It does not matter if the land is called by a different name."

The bleak hollowness that had filled her at the start of the meal all but gone, Cait smiled at Roysa, Idalia, and Sabine. The sisters she'd always wanted but never had. Her eyes swelled with tears.

"I am thankful for each of you," she said. "Grateful to have been brought into your lives."

It would be beyond cruel if the extended family she'd only just found was torn away from her so soon. They had to have been welcomed through the city's gates. They had to be okay.

She simply could not entertain the alternative.

CHAPTER 30

"Those walls have been scaled but once, and never successfully. Perhaps we should . . ."

Noreham stopped. He was looking at something over his shoulder.

Conrad waited for him to continue, their talk of preparations to move on London continuing.

"Conrad, look." Lance stood next to Noreham. His expression had been grim for most of the morn. But not now. The blacksmith actually smiled.

Turning to the open flap of the tent in which they had gathered, Conrad could not believe what he was seeing. It could not be . . .

They'd given up hope for it.

"'Tis gone."

The Plantagenet banner, the red and gold that had been taunting them all morn, was, indeed, gone.

He did not hesitate.

"Now," he shouted. "We ride now!"

His words were met with cheers, but they could not celebrate just yet. There was much that could still go wrong. And yet, it felt like a sign the tide had turned, once again, in their favor.

"The banner is gone," he said to Guy, almost in wonder.

Guy clapped him on the back. "'Tis good news, my friend."

They shouted orders to their men, getting them mobilized, and then ran to their mounts. Conrad waited impatiently as his squires fixed his arming cap into place, his helm and gloves the only two items he had to put on as they'd all been suited much earlier that morn.

His men knew their positions.

They had all prepared for this.

Mounted, he waited for the others. Lance, Guy, Terric . . . they would ride alongside him in the lead, as agreed. None hesitated. If they were to take the city unawares during mass, they didn't have much time.

Charging down the mountain, ahead of all other men, and watching the twin towers of Aldgate loom closer and closer, Conrad said a silent prayer, summoning the strength, if not the impetuousness and temperament, of his father.

Together, they would seize a different path, a different future for England. Conrad would face worse odds for Cait. For Licheford.

With only the slightest of pauses, Conrad rode over the drawbridge and into the city whose gates were, indeed, open and unmanned, side by side with his brothers, who'd formed an order that could have gotten each of them killed for being traitors.

Still could, but it seemed less likely with every passing moment. Not only were the gates unmanned, but it was as if a plague had spread through this section of London. Conrad did not know how their supporters within the city gates had managed it, but they'd not spotted one person yet.

Nay, that was incorrect.

There were two, actually. And he knew one of them, though not the companion, well.

FitzWalter rode toward them.

That he was not armored told Conrad all he needed to know. Yanking off his gloves and helm, he addressed the southern leader of their rebellion as he rode toward them.

"'Tis a relief to see you."

"Pardon the delay," FitzWalter shouted back. Shouting was necessary, for the mounted men who entered Aldgate behind them were anything but silent.

Guy laughed beside him, and Conrad could not blame him. They'd almost attacked the greatest city in England because of that "delay."

"A story for another time," FitzWalter said. "Do the men know their positions?"

Even as he spoke, the men riding behind them began fanning out in different directions. They all had their part to play, a plan they'd fine-tuned over the last few days. Within minutes, the entirety of London would be occupied. When John's supporters realized as much, there *would* be bloodshed that day.

Their work had only begun, but he felt assured of their success.

"They do." He nodded to the others, only Guy without a helm as was his custom. Without another word, all four departed, Conrad raising a fist in parting to FitzWalter. "You've done well," he shouted, riding past him.

"'Tis your turn," he heard from behind.

Indeed it was. More than fifty knights followed him, their destination, Westminster. Soon, church bells would ring, the streets would be flooded with people, noble and common, and they would all learn what he and his supporters knew already.

London had been seized by rebels. If the king refused to meet their demands, Louis, the son of King Philip, could sail unopposed up the Thames to the very abbey Conrad sat in front of now. The one that hosted the coronation of England's kings.

The future of London, of England, was now theirs.

CHAPTER 31

"R iders," Idalia cried, running into the hall. "Riders have been spotted just outside the gates."

"How many?" Cait asked, jumping from her seat so quickly the edge of her sleeve dipped into the bowl of stew in front of her.

Eight nights they had been gone, each of them worse than the last.

As Cait hastily attempted to clean her sleeve, the others abandoned her to the task. A maidservant handed her a linen serviette, and Cait took it with shaking hands, too flustered to do much with it. The girl took the serviette back, dipped it in a goblet of water on their table, and completed the task for her.

With a grateful smile, she closed her eyes and took a deep breath. She was eager to join the others, but a part of her hesitated to do so. She feared what they might have learned. Even so, she'd learned the steep cost of avoidance. She thanked the girl and slowly made her way outside of the keep and into the courtyard.

Her heart lurched at the looks on the other women's faces.

"What is it?"

Sabine spoke first. "They say there are only a few riders. Four men."

"That . . . that cannot be." Why so few? What did it mean? Where were the others, the hundreds who had ridden out? "No, that cannot be," she repeated.

Cait looked to Roysa, but she did not appear any more inclined to offer an explanation than the others.

Four men.

Though darkness had just begun to fall, Cait fixed her gaze on the long pathway leading away from the castle. She watched it, as did they all, for any kind of movement. The courtyard filled with curious on-lookers, the steward included. But still, no riders.

She could not breathe. This was just like waiting in Dromsley Hall during the battle—looking for her brother, searching each face with mingled hope and dread. Only now she also awaited news of Conrad.

And then he rode into view—a magnificent figure of a man astride a massive destrier. He loomed large and imposing, just like he had upon her arrival at Licheford weeks before, but there was a difference this time.

Before, Conrad had seemed shocked, although not altogether pleased, to see her.

This time, he smiled.

She quickly scanned the others but did not recog-nize any of the men.

"Terric?" she called as the others questioned Conrad at the same time. Although he was riding to-ward them quickly, his horse kicking up dust in his haste to get to them, he did not wait to speak. Maybe he could see the worry in their faces.

"All is well," he shouted. "London is ours. I'm here to bring you to them."

The screaming was not just her own. Roysa and Idalia hugged as cheers erupted from all around them. But Cait only had one thing on her mind.

She ran toward Conrad, and by the time she reached him, he had dismounted. He gathered her in his arms and kissed her, not stopping even when whooping and clapping erupted from the courtyard. Only when she broke away to ensure his words were true did the cheers cease.

"Terric is well?"

Conrad nodded, handing the reins of his horse to a stableboy. When a second moved to help the first, Conrad stopped him.

"Will you take this?" he asked, removing his gloves. "And this?" He removed his light armor with the boy's help as Cait and the others watched in confusion.

"A bath, if you please," he called to the steward, who immediately disappeared into the keep.

Conrad smiled at her as Cait finally realized what he was doing.

"I regret I'm unable to give you a full accounting," he said to the others, looking at Sabine, who smiled back at him as a sister would. "The men will do so for me. I can tell you this, London is ours. The cause has been won."

"Won?" Sabine asked, her eyes wide. "Do you mean . . . ?"

"King John will meet us in six days' time at Runnymede."

Cait was too stunned to respond.

"Meet you?" Sabine mumbled. Cait could tell her friend fought off tears. This rebellion was as important to her as it was to any member of the order. Her parents had died fighting the king's unjust policies—

her father was one of the original dissenters who had paid the ultimate price.

"Aye," Conrad said, taking Cait's hand. "Within days of learning of our occupation of London, he took all of his provisions to Bramber Castle. Having lost the treasury and Exchequer at Westminster, he had no choice, really. We received letters of safe passage just before I left to come here. We meet with him on the fifteenth of June."

Cait's heart raced.

"We," he repeated. "All of us. I've come to escort you all there."

When Conrad looked to her, Cait knew what this meant. His barely perceptible nod confirmed it. It had been his idea to come for them. To include them.

To include her.

"The men will explain in greater detail. But prepare to ride out in the morn."

"The men?" Roysa asked. "Why do you keep saying that? Where are you . . ."

She stopped, realizing Conrad's intent. At the same moment, Cait's hand was tugged in the direction of the keep. And then he lifted her into his arms, the women bursting into giggles behind them.

"Will you join me for a bath?"

"Is the choice mine?" she asked, pretending not to notice the looks they were getting as they passed through the courtyard.

"Nay," he admitted. "'Tis not."

All the way to their chamber, Cait pressed her head to his chest, listening to his heartbeat, assuring herself he was alive and all was well. She felt safe for the first time in days, partly because *he* was safe.

"Is that smile for me?"

He put her down just before opening the door.

Though there were not as many candles as there'd

been the night of their wedding, the servants had arranged the large wooden tub just before the fire, in the very spot where they'd first made love.

Conrad set his sword on the sole table in the room, and Cait's eyes followed his fingers as he untied the leather belt at his waist. She sighed, actually sighed, when he took off his surcoat and tunic, revealing his sculpted body.

"Yours," he said, continuing to undress. "This is yours. I am yours. Everything you see is yours, Cait. It has been, always."

Before she could think of a proper response to words that both dried her throat and made her pulse quicken, her husband was in the tub. Grabbing the soap that sat on a wooden stool next to him, he disappeared into the water. Cait took off her gown and then her shift.

If she had thought Conrad handsome before, he looked even more so as he emerged from the water and slicked back his wet hair. When his eyes found her, Cait's heartbeat raced even more.

The way he looked at her . . .

Shoulders back, as proud as if she wore the most fashionable gown at court, Cait strode to the tub. Under his gaze, Cait felt more powerful than she ever had in her life. There was no mistaking the hunger in his eyes.

For her.

She did not wait for him to ask. Instead, Cait stepped up onto the wooden stool beside the tub. Conrad reached up to take her hand and guided her into the tub. Though it was nearly as cramped as the first time, it somehow felt right that their reunion should be here.

Without a word, he guided her leg to one side, and she straddled him. This conqueror of kings, very much in Cait's control, both of them consumed by the same need.

Without a word, Cait leaned down. Conrad's hand snaked through the hair at the nape of her neck. Grabbing a handful of it, he pulled her down the rest of the way until their lips met. His mouth slanted over hers, covering it completely. Every bit of him demanded. And Cait was happy to meet those demands.

Reaching beneath the water, she tested her special powers and was rewarded with a moan from Conrad that vibrated against her lips. When his hand covered hers, both of them guiding him into her, Cait cursed herself for having waited so long to come to him.

Better to treasure what we have now than bemoan what we've lost.

And she did treasure him.

As he slid in and out, Conrad massaged her buttocks with his hands, every bit of Cait bursting with pleasure. Reveling in the heat of the fire next to them, the heat created between.

The slow lovemaking became a frenzy of tangled limbs and splashed water. Even more so than the first time, their joining signified the end of a very long journey as two separated people became one.

"It feels so good," she said, breaking away reluctantly but needing some sort of temporary reprieve from the sensations that threatened to overwhelm her.

"I love you, Cait."

As if reinforcing the tenderly stated words, Conrad thrust into her, and Cait did not hold back. She met him, hips circling in the rhythm they'd created, thrust for thrust. She wanted to say the words back, but no sound came from her.

At least, none that formed coherent words.

When Conrad's jaw clenched at the same time as the muscles in his shoulders flexed, the sheer power of her husband coupled with the very gentle way he held her hips . . . Cait could not hold on any longer.

"Conrad . . ."

With one final thrust, Cait finally let go. The power, regret, love, pleasure . . . all of it mingled between them as she cried out his name.

Her entire body shuddered as Conrad's head fell back against the side of the tub. Collapsing atop him, Cait somehow managed to hold her head just above the water.

With his help.

"I cannot move," she said finally. "Nor do I wish to just yet."

Conrad pushed a strand of her hair behind her ears.

"If we stayed in this tub forever, I would die a happy man."

Cait smiled. "That may very well be true. But I think you would have a difficult time explaining to Terric why you did not appear at Runnymede."

Conrad sighed. "I suppose you are correct."

She pulled off of him and began to move away when he stopped her.

"Just one more moment."

As he looked at her, a question in his eyes, Cait realized what her husband waited for, and she said the words gladly.

"I love you too. Always."

CHAPTER 32

R unnymede, England, 15 June 1215
"Will you come with us?" Conrad
asked.

Cait had just entered their tent to fetch a mantle for protection against the cold. They'd been in this open meadow between Windsor and Staines for just over a sennight, the negotiations having taken longer than anyone had expected. Last eve, however, just after the sun had set, the men had come back with the happy news.

It was done.

They'd finally agreed on all sixty clauses of the Charter of Runnymede, and it was being readied for them to sign. And although the king had returned to Windsor Castle each night rather than stay in this tent city that had been erected, he would be present this morn.

"I am not needed," she said to her husband, grateful for the invitation nonetheless.

When his hands slipped around her waist, Cait leaned into him, enjoying a warmth more profound than any mantle could give her. Would she ever become accustomed to her husband's closeness? When he was near, she had difficulty thinking of little else besides his touch.

"*I* need you."

He brushed her hair aside with his chin, his lips finding her neck. Cait tilted her head to the side to give him better access.

"You do not," she chided, Cait's core clenching as he kissed just under her ear. She swallowed.

What were they discussing?

His tongue?

Nay, their meeting with the king.

"Conrad—"

He spun her around, his lips capturing hers. As he kissed her, Conrad took the mantle from her hands and slid it over her shoulders. She felt the warmth of the soft fabric enveloping her. Much as Conrad was doing with his arms.

Cait would have been content to remain as such for the entire day, but . . .

"You've a treaty to sign." She pulled away reluctantly.

He would not be swayed. After securing her mantle, he took her hand and kissed her once more. "Come."

When they stepped outside, Cait startled. The others were all there, already mounted. Lance and Idalia, Guy and Sabine, Terric and Roysa . . .

"Apologies." Conrad guided her toward them. "We had a slight delay."

Judging from their expressions, they knew precisely what Conrad meant by "delay." She could feel her cheeks warming.

"I did not realize you would all . . ." She let her sentence drift off. Conrad, Terric, Guy, and Lance all bore the mark of the fleur-de-lis, as did Sabine. The mark of the Order of the Broken Blade. Just yesterday Conrad had suggested that perhaps she would like to get the same mark once they returned to Licheford.

Only now did she realize what he'd truly been asking. He wanted her to join the order. She could only be an honorary member, truly, because she was no knight.

But even so . . .

"Will you come with us?" Conrad asked again.

"Of course," she said as his squire and another page brought their horses forward. "Of course," she mumbled again, through a throat clogged with emotion. For years, she'd felt weighed down by the guilt of what had happened. By the fact that Conrad bore a scar because of her. That he had been forced to kill a man, a king's man, because of her. That her brother had become a man driven by revenge, because of her.

But she'd lost sight of the fact that these four men had come together, in part, because of her. By asking her to join them, Conrad was telling her that she had played a role in their victory.

Once she and Conrad were settled on their mounts, her husband nodded to the others and told them they were ready. Riding away from the tent city, Cait was lulled into a near trance. Her mind wandered back to that day, to everything that had happened since . . .

"I am one of you," she said firmly.

"You are one of us," Conrad confirmed. They rode at the lead, the others following behind them, two by two. "The most important one of us."

A bird called out to them, as if signaling the way toward the king. He would be there. The king would be at this meeting. It was not an ordinary occurrence, to be sure.

"This day would have come without me, or Terric."

Conrad shrugged his shoulders. "Perhaps. Or perhaps not."

Cait turned in her saddle, catching her brother's eye behind them. Terric winked at her.

"I can hardly believe this is happening." And it was true. It was as if she rode in someone else's body.

"I will admit, I feared it would come to naught. Even yesterday one of the king's clerics returned to the negotiations with a message from the king that could have easily sent both sides home without a treaty. Negotiations continued, thankfully, and eventually prevailed."

Cait took in a deep breath, the crisp morning air a perfect complement to the mood among them. Hopeful, but hesitant too.

"Roysa seems particularly happy that widows will not be forced to remarry in order to keep their property," she said.

"Your brother insisted on that particular clause."

"And you, which are you most pleased with of them all?"

Conrad thought for a bit. Cait was content to just ride alongside him, pretending, most unsuccessfully, they were simply out for a morning ride.

"No scutage nor aid is to be imposed on the kingdom except by the common counsel of the kingdom."

It was the article he'd fought for most this past year, and Cait was proud that such language was included in the treaty. She was proud of him.

"You are quite a man, Conrad, Earl of Licheford."

What was once a white speck in the distance suddenly loomed before them. Unlike the rebels' camp, there were only a few tents, one of which clearly belonged to the king. Had Cait been walking, she might have faltered. Thankfully, her mount kept moving forward.

She realized Conrad watched her. Realized they had slowed enough for the others to ride up beside them. Terric had fallen in at her left, Roysa beside him, and Lance and Idalia rode beyond them. Guy's mount was to Conrad's right, Sabine sitting tall and proud on her own horse, staring at King John's tent as if she meant to tear it to the ground.

None spoke for a time, until Conrad finally broke the silence.

"Shall we finish it, then?"

In answer, they moved forward together.

The Order of the Broken Blade.

EPILOGUE

"He said nothing of why we are here?" Conrad asked the others. They had been back at Licheford for two days. On the morrow, his friends would leave with their wives.

Idalia was the only one among them who seemed to know why Lance had requested this gathering. When he had asked to meet privately, Conrad had surprised everyone, including himself, by asking for his father's solar to be prepared.

The request had startled Wyot, but his face had split into a huge grin. The steward had been advising him to take up residence in it since his parents' death, insisting the earl's rightful place was here, in this chamber.

The servants had done their job well, for it looked just as it had the last time he'd been in here, years before. His mother's touch was everywhere. Her affinity for weaving and bright colors was on display in every tapestry. He could hardly spy a bit of stone for the coverings.

I should have come here sooner.

Conrad realized his wife was watching him, likely knowing the direction of his thoughts. He took advantage of their position on the intricately carved bench and slid even closer to her. All but Lance and Idalia were present, sitting on a bench opposite them.

"I will be sitting on your lap soon," she whispered.

"An intriguing thought," he said, moving to lift her into such a position when the door opened.

The first thing he noticed was Lance's face. A broad smile was not his friend's typical expression. He had something planned, but Conrad could not imagine what that might be.

He noticed, then, that Lance carried a sword. Why would he have drawn his . . .

It was not just any sword. Although Lance's hand covered the hilt, Conrad had a clear look at the guard as his friend came closer. Nondescript, he recognized it anyway. Could it be?

Nay, that sword lay at the bottom of a river.

The chamber was so silent when Lance presented it to him, Conrad could hear his friend's breathing. He stood, accepting it, still not understanding.

"I went back," Lance explained. "Worried it could be found, could implicate you if identified."

The smaller training sword had been no match for Cait's attacker, but it had saved them in the end. It was the sharp edge of the broken blade that Conrad had used to stab him. To kill him.

"I kept it, reforged it . . ."

Conrad looked from the sword up to Lance. He nodded.

Unsheathing it, the sound reverberating through the silent chamber, Conrad gasped. A new blade, but unlike the original. Fleurs-de-lis, like the ones all eight of them in this room now bore, were engraved down its length. It was the most spectacular piece of craftsmanship Conrad had ever seen.

"You put it back together," he said finally, not

knowing what surprised him more—that Lance had recovered it and kept it a secret or that he'd somehow found the time to forge this exquisite piece.

"The sword, aye. But us?" His hands swept the room. Conrad did not dare look at Cait if he thought to keep his composure. "You did that. And I will be forever grateful to you for it."

He hadn't noticed Guy and Terric rising from their seats. But suddenly all four stood in a circle, looking at Lance's work. Guy nodded, pleased.

Terric clasped him on the shoulder with one hand and extended his arm, fist clenched, into the center of their group with the other.

Lance did not hesitate to clasp his wrist.

Then Guy.

And finally Conrad, sheathing the sword and completing their circle.

"We took a vow of silence," Terric said. "And then another to form an order that includes more than just the four of us."

Conrad did look back then.

Cait's eyes glimmered with unshed tears, but she was smiling. No longer the scared young woman he had met that day, but a strong and beautiful one who had been through so much to sit here with them in this chamber.

He loved her even more than he loved these men, these brothers. He'd give his life for any of them, if necessary. Turning back to them now, he looked at each one in turn.

His brother-in-law, ever the protector.

Guy, who grinned even now, making it near impossible not to join him.

And Lance. Although he'd only been knighted this past year, he lived the code more fully than anyone who'd been raised to fulfill such a role.

"Today," Terric finished, "we make another. To remember that all we've fought for means nothing without each other. Without them."

Their wives. The women who completed each of them.

"To the order," Guy said.

Conrad swallowed, his throat thick with love and pride. "The Order of the Broken Blade."

AUTHOR'S NOTE

I typically reserve the history behind a series for my reader group, but this time the order compelled me to share right here. Although it is always an integral part of my stories, for the Order of the Broken Blade, the history actually became a character, woven into the first chapter of book one until the very last paragraphs of *The Earl*. The significance of these characters' actions carried a weight, a responsibility, I took seriously.

The Magna Carta.

When I first viewed this historical document on a visit to Salisbury Cathedral, I understood I stood in the presence of something monumental. A document that changed the course of history. As I began researching for this series, learning about twenty-five barons who had dared to rebel against a corrupt king, I wondered about the document itself and the people who had brought it about.

After all, it's no small feat to rebel against a king.

Although not much of a rulebreaker, I did disobey my own mother on an occasion or two, a scary enough proposition that makes me shudder at the very idea of disobeying a man such as King John, or

"Lackland" as he was known by his contemporaries. I could write an entire appendix just about the man himself. Brother to Richard the Lionheart, with whom he did not get along, King John was implicated in the murder of his nephew and was accused of trying to rape the daughter of one of his barons.

In short, a perfect villain.

His rule was so poorly received, twenty-five barons, as represented by the four men at the core of our story, revolted against him. It was only when they took London, as described in *The Earl*, that King John agreed to sign the Articles of the Barons. Unfortunately, he later reneged, asking Pope Innocent III to declare it invalid. This began a civil conflict that became known later as the First Barons' War.

When John died in the midst of the war, our rebellious barons, led by Robert FitzWalter and a French army under the future Louis VIII of France, continued to fight. The articles signed by our order in *The Earl* later became what we now know as the Magna Carta. Eventually, Louis suffered multiple defeats, our barons switched sides with John now dead, and the Treaty of Lambeth was signed on 11 September 1217. The rebel barons, according to one of the provisions of the treaty, were offered amnesty.

Although the characters in the Order of the Broken Blade are all fictional, I drew inspiration for many of them from real people. Sabine's father, for instance, was based on a man accused in 1212, alongside Lord Robert FitzWalter, of plotting against John's life.

Terric's mother was based on the story of Edward of Salisbury, a man who supported the rebels after the king seized his lordship. Trowbridge became Dromsley and one of Terric's motivations to rebel against King John.

Perhaps my favorite story is the one of Robert FitzWalter, who was actually the leader of the baronial rebellion against John. One particular account gave me inspiration for Conrad's hardheaded father.

"According to the Histoire des ducs de Normandie, Robert once sprang to the defence of his son-in-law when the latter killed a serving man in a dispute over lodgings at court and John threatened to hang him, declaring 'By God's body, you will not hang my son-in-law, you'll see two hundred lanced knights in your land before you hang him!' When the king put the case up for trial, FitzWalter appeared in court with two hundred knights."

There are so many factual tidbits, it is impossible to share them all. But if you find this particular era as fascinating as I did, visit The Magna Carta Trust, whose website, which celebrates 800 years of Magna Carta history, was one of my most utilized resources and from which I took the quote about FitzWarren above.

Winston Churchill once described the Magna Carta as "the foundation of principles and systems of government of which neither King John or his nobles dreamed." Little did he know it would inspire four men, friends since childhood, to find love and change the course of history, at least in this author's fantastical mind.

Printed in Poland
by Amazon Fulfillment
Poland Sp. z o.o., Wrocław

53741360R00127